GW01191101

FAITHLESS UNTO DEATH!

A Detective Inspector Ken Jones Mystery

Paul Cosway

The Kingston Press

ISBN-13: 979880162536
ISBN-10: 1477123456

Cover design by: Art Painter
Library of Congress Control Number: 2018675309
Printed in the United States of America

FAITHLESS UNTO DEATH

'Let me tell you about the very rich. They are different from you and me.' (F Scott Fitzgerald 1896 - 1940)

'Yes, they have more money.' (Ernest Hemingway 1899 - 1961}

◆ ◆ ◆

◆ ◆ ◆

We Begin...

Olivia sipped from her glass of perfectly chilled Chablis and smiled at her four friends. 'No woman,' she declared, 'should be arrested for killing her husband!' Her friends gasped in delighted astonishment. Nikki put down her wine glass and applauded.
'Bloody true! They're a bloody pain!'

Olivia nodded and smiled. As she moved, the sequins on her Ralph Lauren gun metal cocktail dress shimmered in the light from the floor to ceiling windows. Her eyes were shrewd, more than capable of assessing the cost of every outfit worn by her friends, but less skilled, perhaps, at judging people. 'A bloody pain, yes! There may be one or two worth holding on to...' she conceded, but gaze under the carefully applied mascara and see the doubt in her eyes. Nikki's husband was a possible exception. She had tried him out and his performance between the sheets had convinced her he was wasted on Nikki. She stared hard at her friend. Nikki was wearing a Ted Baker midi dress in orange with a large white and blue flower printed on the skirt. The flaring from the waist set off her hips and long legs, though Olivia knew that her impossibly high stiletto heels added a much needed six inches to her limbs. The whole outfit would have set her back, Olivia reckoned, around three hundred pounds. Good on the outside, but Olivia had long thought there was something, well, common about Nikki. She pressed home her point. 'Oh yes. It's all chocolates and roses at first. But once the honeymoon's over, they're just trouble. If women were in charge, killing your husband would automatically be classed as justifiable homicide!'

Olivia's liking for American crime dramas maybe led to her confusing US law with that of her own country. There is no defence of justifiable homicide in British law. The equivalent is 'lawful killing', which would hardly apply in this case. But Olivia was simply making a general point – that husbands were often such a nuisance – so annoying – that the mere fact that one was married to one should be enough to justify the use of cyanide. She felt confident among these women – her closest friends. They wouldn't take offence or misjudge her. She could trust them even with her most extreme views. As far as one could trust anyone. She waited for their reaction, and she wasn't disappointed. Her listeners laughed with delight. Solid gold bracelets jingled, as immaculately manicured fingers held tightly to their hand-cut lead crystal wine goblets. On one perfect, elegant neck, four strings of pearls shimmered. Beautifully botoxed faces creased into delighted smiles. Expensively coiffured hair rose and sank in time to their laughter. Complete agreement.

One of her well-heeled guests, Emma, (Ashoki midi dress in a black and white print, with flared skirt and black strappy sandals. From Monsoon, Olivia guessed. Looked good on Emma, but quite cheap. Like Emma. Olivia believed that she could tell everything about people from the clothes they wore. All that was worth knowing, anyway.) Emma waved a glass of gin and tonic carefully round. She was taking in the room, with its expensive, custom-made curtains; the rare antique porcelain; the tasteful and enormously expensive works of art that adorned the walls. 'After he's paid for everything, I hope!' Emma joked. Like the others, she knew exactly where their wealth came from. They were trophy wives, honest enough to admit it wasn't their husbands' looks that had first attracted them. It was their money. Their power. Their status. And it wasn't business acumen that had made these men wealthy. They had inherited money. Rather than being born and bred they were born and cake. And, in turn, it wasn't these women's intellects that had made them desirable wives. No – they were attractive accessories. Something beautiful these men could use to show the world how successful they are. 'Look at me! Look at this gorgeous creature who thinks I'm so amazing she's married me!' For the women, of course, it meant they had to keep their looks. A trophy is no use to anyone once it's tarnished. Emma pushed the point home. 'Make bloody sure you've fleeced them for all they've got before you do 'em in!'

The others nodded in agreement – they would have applauded her if they could have done so without spilling their drinks onto the soft, luxurious sofas on which they decorously perched.

'Well of course!' the hostess agreed. 'Do you think I'm mad? Milk them for all they're worth first!' Four heads nodded in agreement: their eyelashes perfect, make-up immaculate. They sank further into the chairs, two with their elegant legs crossed, the others with them angled demurely, Princess Diana style. Yes, essential to make sure first that they were set up for life. Although they'd never admit it, even to each other, they knew they were prizes. Adornments to their men's lives. They could easily have married men more physically attractive, but that would have led to a much poorer lifestyle. No. The popular song put it so well – when it comes down to it, diamonds are a girl's best friend. And if the lucky man you've chosen as a partner isn't as romantic as you would ideally wish – there's always the chance for a little adventure on the side. After all, they were away on business so much...

Olivia's lips curled up into a smile, as genuine as the ones she practised so often in her mirror (to ensure that she could express her delight without a trace of a line or - heaven forbid - a wrinkle). It was a smile directed towards Nikki that had two quite separate meanings. On a superficial level it whispered, 'Yes, you and I are so alike. We both understand that to own all this, without the encumbrance of the men who go with it, would be oh so desirable.' On a deeper level, below the carefully applied foundation and the eyeshadow and the silk lingerie, a deeper voice whispered, 'I've seen you. The secret kiss on New Year's Eve; the imperceptible glimpse of a car key you thought no-one would notice; the lightest of touches on your behind as my husband slipped past you; Nikki you snake.' It was a smile that meant we are the closest of friends. And revenge, when it comes, will be all the sweeter...

Olivia enjoyed these get-togethers every Thursday. They took it in turns to play hostess. But she liked them best when her turn came around. She loved her status as the head of the group. Hers was the largest home, the most luxurious - in its own parkland, just outside Sherborne. She could boast of more bathrooms than she had bedrooms – and there were more than enough of those. Her kitchen had all the finest, most expensive German gadgets – which, of course, she never used. The white goods in the utility room (larger than many a living room) looked as if they had never been touched, because they never had. What's the point of laundries if you never use them? The best caterers had been called in to supply the finger food for this get together – caviar, smoked salmon, tiny canapes (all very expensive and barely touched. One had to watch one's figure after all). And the caterers had to work from a large van outside, not even allowed on the drive. They had to put sheets of cloth down as they walked in and out so there was no chance they would soil the perfect carpets. And those coverings had to be rolled up and back in the van before the first guests arrived.

The ladies had almost finished the second bottle of Chablis, each one of which cost as much as a normal family would spend on food for a week. Olivia had to maintain her position. She was the envy of the others, even though each one was disgustingly wealthy. Every week they had to buy new outfits for this one occasion. It would have been unthinkable to appear in anything they had been seen in before. The first few minutes of each session would be spent swooning over each other's appearance. They would discuss designer labels and expensive fabrics the way others, less fortunate, would chat about the weather.

The wine was having a mellowing effect. The world was looking rosier by the minute. And the prospect, which Olivia had offered, of being able to enjoy all this without the necessary encumbrance of a husband was tempting indeed. And speaking of husbands, Nikki felt obliged to ask, 'David's in

France, isn't he? Weren't you tempted to join him and enjoy a short break yourself – good food, good wine…?'

Olivia rolled her eyes in horror at the prospect. 'He's in Brittany! Staying in an Ibis or something equally horrid!! It's hardly Monte Carlo, is it?' Nikki clutched Olivia's hand in a gesture of total understanding. No indeed, it was hardly Monte Carlo.

'But he'll have called you…'

Olivia smiled in derision. 'It'll never even cross his mind, even assuming he's sober!' Her guests nodded sympathetically.

Detective Inspector Ken Jones was still struggling to understand why, as a Dorset officer, he had been ordered to board a police helicopter outside Portsmouth to fly out to sea in the middle of the night. An icy cold night with a biting wind. The moon appeared intermittently between huge black clouds, then disappeared just as rapidly, as if turning away from the dark world beneath. He protested in vain to Sergeant Jenny Grace, his assistant: 'I don't trust copters. What if the engine fails? We'd drop like a stone!'

'Don't worry, boss. You're more likely to be hit by a car than be in a helicopter crash.'

Ken mused on this. 'If a car comes at me, I can jump out of the way. Can't jump away from a helicopter.'

Jenny smiled. 'Don't be scared. I'll hold your hand!' And she wouldn't mind doing just that. 'Think yourself lucky. The Hampshire lads had to go out to the ferry on the coastguard's boat in a force six gale. I heard they were all sick as dogs!'

Ken gave a grunt in response. It was his bad luck that the man who had been killed was not only a resident of Dorset, but one of the richest men in the county. He'd be expected to front the enquiries in his own force's area. Normally he'd be happy to help his colleagues in another force. He'd just finished a joint investigation that had meant work in Bristol and Leicester. But flying at night over a rough sea in the pitch dark? No thank you.

One of the pilots waved them forward. He was screaming over the roar of the rotor blades. 'Clear to fly now, sir! Lucky the wind's dropped! We're on the cusp – but it's just about safe enough to risk it! Welcome aboard!'

Reluctantly, Ken took his arm and was helped into the helicopter. Jenny followed, amused by the anxiety felt by her normally unflappable boss. They were strapped in, and the copter rose a few feet into the air. Then it was caught by a sudden gust of wind that made it lurch to one side. Ken felt he was choking and struggled to regain his breath. Jenny clutched his hand. He squeezed her fingers hard, pretending he was reassuring her when actually it was the other way round. The co-pilot turned and smiled broadly. 'Sorry about that, sir. We'll be up above the weather soon!' Ken gave a grim smile in return and wondered what the ride would be like when they dropped down onto the ferry. How would they exit the copter? Would they be winched down, in a howling gale, onto a wildly tossing ship? He was glad he hadn't asked. It was better not to know.

The helicopter soared, like a bird, high into the sky. Suddenly they were above the clouds. He could see millions of stars, far clearer than they had ever seemed from the ground. Below them the clouds looked like sheets of dark grey cotton wool. It was hard to believe that, down there, a storm was still raging. The roar of the engine had muted to a hum. Ken began to relax. For the first time in weeks, he felt calm. He was like an eagle flying high, leaving all his problems on the ground below. Just for a moment they faded away: his distrust of the Assistant Chief Constable, Alicia; the IOPC investigation into his exposure of corrupt police officers; his romance issues with Sheila – whom he once loved and maybe had let down. And there was Jenny at his side. He felt more guilt over her. Had he wronged her? He shouldn't have slept with her, he knew. It had seemed so inconsequential at the time. Too much to drink had led to a one-night stand. But he hadn't mentioned it after. He'd just ignored her, as if it had meant nothing. This was the moment, perhaps, to begin to make amends. He turned to face her, just as the pilot made this announcement.

'We're immediately above the ferry now. Beginning our descent!'

Ken opened his mouth to ask how they would leave the copter and get onto the deck, but then they dropped a couple of hundred feet at speed, leaving his stomach still up with the stars. He was overcome for a moment with nausea. Jenny seemed to be taking this much better than he was. He realised he was still clutching her hand. She squeezed his palm reassuringly as they continued to fall from the sky. Then there was shuddering bump. He gasped. A crash? Jenny smiled at him. 'We've landed.'

He was confused. How could they land a helicopter on a ferry? And as he looked round at the inside of the metallic shell that had brought him here safely, his views on copters changed. It felt familiar and safe. What awaited him when he stepped out onto the deck?

Olivia's four guests were leaving, their taxis waiting on the spacious drive. The maid helped them on with their coats. The rain had stopped but there was a touch of wind chill in the air. Too much for their delicate complexions. Nikki was the last to leave. Her platinum blonde hair was perfectly in place. It looked soft to the touch and glistened as it reflected the light from the inset spotlights in the ceiling. Not a single root gave away her true colour. The breeze pressed the light fabric of her dress against her skin, revealing a lack of underwear. It would have spoilt the line. Her face, Olivia judged, maybe a little unfairly, was pretty, rather than beautiful. She decided that Nikki lacked the fine bone structure that was so much a feature of her own classic profile – but it suited Olivia to criticise everyone, even her friends. A casual observer might disagree. Nikki had her admirers. Olivia's husband, David, had flirted with Nikki outrageously at their last New Year celebration. But she had put it down to an excess of very good champagne. And anyway, her attention had been focused elsewhere. She too had been flirting. More successfully, it had turned out.

Before sliding elegantly into her taxi, Nikki leaned forward and placed a slender hand (with nails that looked almost real, in a shade of pink that matched her lips perfectly) onto Olivia's arm, conspiratorially. 'What you said,' she whispered, 'about doing away with your husband...you weren't really serious, were you?'

Olivia's mouth gave the just the suggestion of a smile. 'Try me!' She knew Nikki had issues with Michael. He'd confessed to Olivia that they never slept together now. Olivia knew that was a waste. She had, well, first hand evidence of his heterosexual prowess... But he had given his wife grief, along with considerable wealth. One, Olivia thought, should cancel out the other. But maybe Nikki wanted free.

Nikki leaned closer. 'But how could it be done? How could you get away with it? Be certain...?'

'Oh, there are ways.'

But just then the taxi driver sounded his horn in impatience. Nikki wound up the window. 'Well – we'll stay in touch, yes?'
Olivia nodded. Nikki wondered. Would the crazy woman really do it? What fun! Yes, she'd keep in touch!

'Bend over as you walk away – I don't want you catching your heads on the rotor blades!' Ken nodded. He didn't fancy being decapitated.

He was almost on all fours as he staggered from the helicopter towards an open doorway on the upper deck. He was astonished at the size of the ship. It even had a helicopter landing pad. His previous experience of ferries had been restricted to crossing to the Isle of Wight on a tiny car ferry. A few metres away from them was a watertight door. It opened to reveal a small welcoming party. The first to step forward was a small but stern woman, around five feet two in height and stocky in build. She had black hair cut short in a no-nonsense fashion and was wearing a very impressive uniform, emblazoned with shiny buttons and gold braid. An officer Ken recognised from the Hampshire force jumped ahead to make the introductions. He didn't want Ken to underestimate the lady in front of him. 'Hello Ken. This is the captain. Marie Fabonne.'

The lady in question stood with her legs slightly apart, either to assert her authority or to retain her balance on the gently rocking ship – Ken wasn't sure. She spoke excellent English with a charming French accent.

'Monsieur Jones. Monsieur Detective. Bienvenue a bord. You are welcome aboard the Pont-Aven!'

Ken's schoolboy French was rusty, but he knew it's polite to try to speak at least a little of the language. 'Merci madame! Le Pont-Aven est tres grand!' And it was indeed more like a cruise ship than a cross channel ferry.

'Merci monsieur. We have much pride in her. She is the finest vessel of our fleet. I will be most happy to take you on tour.'

The Hampshire man cut in. 'That'll be great, but the urgent thing now is to take Jones to the crime scene.'

The captain nodded her agreement. 'Oui. Sans doute. Our schedule – we have our passengers to consider.'

As D.I. Forbes guided Ken through the door that led to the bridge, and then to the narrow stairs that took them to the first of the passenger decks, he elaborated. 'She's right. The logistics of this are a nightmare. The ship's almost full. Nearly two and half thousand passengers and close to seven hundred cars and lorries. The lorry drivers are giving us plenty of grief. Some have perishable goods on board; all have tight schedules. They've got to get to their destinations, unload, and get back on prebooked crossings. They're going to turn nasty if we can't resolve this soon. And then we've got holiday makers who need to get home to start work in the morning – not to mention another couple of thousand waiting in Portsmouth expecting to board and be shipped to France today.'

Ken's astonishment did not decrease as he passed an indoor swimming pool, a pool bar and then down further stairs to a night club and the Commodore deck. 'Down this corridor,' commanded Forbes and led him to the lounge exclusively for passengers wealthy enough to afford the first class cabins. 'We're using this as our incident room. Make yourselves comfy and we'll bring you up to date.'

Jenny sighed as one of the uniformed police officers used the coffee machine to make them a drink. This officer was, she noted grimly, female. 'Nothing changes,' she thought, sadly. 'It was ever thus.'

But her ruminations on equality, or the lack of it, were cut abruptly short. A member of the crew burst into the room and addressed the captain. She deduced from the line of braid on his sleeve that he was something important. She deduced from the state of him – dishevelled, panting, and red in the face – that something was wrong. 'Les routiers!' he cried. 'A problem! Vite!'

There was a short but animated discussion in French that Jenny did not pretend to understand. Then the lady turned to them. 'A disturbance,' she proclaimed calmly. 'A group of - how do you say it? – lorry drivers, yes? They are demanding that we sail into Portsmouth immediately. They are holding two members of my crew. They are threatening to throw them overboard if we do not agree!'

The British contingent gazed at her in

astonishment. Ken was first to find his voice. 'But they can't be serious! Surely?'

The captain held him with a steady gaze, and her next words were heavy with the experience of many years of dealing with French union members. 'It is obvious you have never had to deal with French lorry drivers.' And she was gone. The proud members of the British police force, left in limbo, gazed at each other helplessly. 'Do you think we should go...back her up?' asked Ken, not sure what to think. Forbes shrugged.

'She seems to know what she's doing. Better just wait and see. If she needs our help, I'm sure she'll ask...'

'Is it a job for the gendarmes?' offered Jenny. 'Them being French and all?'

Forbes dismissed this reluctantly. 'It would help us a lot if we could fly a squad in – but it's a no go. We're only a mile out of Portsmouth, so we're in UK territorial waters. They'd have no jurisdiction here. Best not to interfere at all – unless we're asked to.' General nodding of heads and mental crossing of fingers. They all knew that the six of them could do little if dozens of angry truck drivers turned really nasty.

'Anyway – time we looked over the crime scene, don't you think?' And keen to put the crisis to one side and get on with something they understood, they all agreed, and Forbes led them out of the make-shift incident room into the corridor that led to the murder scene.

◆ ◆ ◆

The Chief Constable leaned back in his leather chair and stared moodily into his glass, admiring the colour of the whisky. Single malt, of course. And from a very good distillery. The Assistant Chief Constable watched him warily from her slightly less comfortable seat. This was their regular weekly get-together. A chance to reflect on progress over the last seven days. And on any problems that had cropped up. And it was a very particular problem that was causing the Chief to stare moodily into his cut crystal tumbler. 'I had high hopes of Jones. He was a breath of fresh air after Longbottom. Even considered him joining the lodge.'

A.C.C. Alicia Conroy crossed her legs, clad in dark blue tights. Her black sensible shoes shone in the light streaming in from the large window with its view across the Dorset hills. This was a sore point for her. As a woman she was not allowed to join the Masons and this she deeply resented. Privately, she thought herself more manly than most members of the lodge. Many of her colleagues on the force would struggle to disagree. But her acidic blue eyes held him with a steady gaze. The hard features of her face, with her chiselled cheekbones, showed not a flicker of regret. Her thin lips attempted a smile and failed. 'I can't pretend that he's always an asset, Chief. He's bright enough. Excellent report on him from Leicester on the work he did to tie up the investigation into forced marriages…'

'Ah! The bodies in the garden! Turned out to be all young girls! Messy business!'

'Cleared up now, as you know. Yes, he's sharp. But he's a loose cannon. A law unto himself. Obsessed with protecting women from abuse. And more – picking up on misogyny in the force. And reporting the perpetrators as soon as he finds them. No referral to higher authority. He follows orders when it suits him. It's like a crusade with him.'

The Chief squinted at her, making sure of his facts before his next statement. 'But surely, you're a woman.' Yes, that was true. 'Thought you might approve of what he's doing.'

'The force comes first, sir. Some things are better covered up. Left for us to deal with. It's bad for morale. And as for this incident with the Met – causing real difficulties. You can tell they're increasingly reluctant to help us.'

A sip of whisky. It warmed his mouth. The world began to look rosier. In turn, Alicia lifted her glass of dry sherry, wet her lips, then lowered it again. The Chief was about to speak. 'Ah yes. Their men got badly beaten up, didn't they? Over a couple of women of the night. But it could have been worse, couldn't it? If Jones and his sergeant hadn't been on hand and intervened?'

Alicia dismissed this with a wave of her hand. The dazzling silver buttons on her uniform flashed brightly, almost blinding the Chief for a second. She was always so immaculately attired that, in her company, he always felt slightly shabby - although he could never quite see why. Many on the force maintained that she never took her uniform off. Even slept in it. Surely not. It would be creased. She spoke decisively. 'That's the line we're taking with the police conduct people. They don't buy it, of course. Not enough evidence, though, for them to make a case. For the moment he's in the clear.'

'And your opinion?'

A sip of sherry. 'Nothing would surprise me. Every time he's involved with men who've abused women, they come to considerable harm. One of those Met men will be in a wheelchair for the rest of his life. If it turned out that he's colluded with those sex workers to ambush two officers so that their minders could beat them senseless – well, it wouldn't be a surprise.'

A raised eyebrow. 'But nothing can be proved?'

'No. As long as the sex workers refuse to name their pimps, he's in the clear. They're standing by Jones.'

'As he stood by them, perhaps?'

'Yes. Precisely.'

'And I suppose the Met men were asking for trouble. They'd only themselves to blame.'

The hatchet face expressed scorn. And expressed it well. It was the emotion it was best suited to. 'They shouldn't have done it. Of course. Completely wrong to demand free sex, under threat of prosecution. But did they deserve what they got? Did that warrant life changing injuries?'

The Chief shook his head sadly. 'Maybe not. Maybe not. But we'll have to be careful. It's made Jones something of a hero.'

It was clear that Alicia felt that hero was overdoing it. 'You've heard about the BBC's interest?'

The Chief closed his eyes in resignation. 'Still going ahead, is it?'

'PR and the Commissioner insist on it. Bloody stupid idea!'

The Chief allowed one weary eye to open and nodded. 'The female-friendly-face of the force, is it? Quite good looking, I suppose. I can see the appeal for the telly people. What do they call it? Photogenic?'

Alicia couldn't see the attraction. But then so many women are, she believed, stupid. Far too impressed by the opposite sex. Men are dangerous creatures. They need watching carefully. 'They're doing a feature on the police's attitude to women. We'll have to be sure we control the agenda!'

The Chief's brain jolted into something approaching a functioning state. 'You think he could blurt out something embarrassing?'

'Of course he could! We need him to say there were a couple of bad apples. They've been removed from duty. The force is clean. That there's no need to worry. But he's only to start mouthing off examples of misconduct: officers taking snapshots of women's naked bodies; male officers demanding sex from sex workers to avoid prosecution; and we're up shit creek!'

The chief sat bolt upright. It was partly because of her language. He wasn't used to women being quite so forceful. But he took her meaning. 'Bloody hell! And without a bleeding paddle! Do you think I should speak to him? Make it clear what he's allowed to say?'

His assistant nodded, but her acid stare implied that she was far from sure her boss was up to it. 'Anything you can do will be valuable of course. I'll make my views clear as well. And we need to ensure that we have a solicitor and PR in attendance at the recording to check everything he says. And we must insist on editorial control. We mustn't allow anything to be broadcast that could cause us any embarrassment!'

The Chief nodded furiously. 'Organise all that will you, Alicia? That should cover it! Good work!' And with that he poured himself another whisky. A double. 'Sooner we get on to it the better. Where's Jones now?'

Alicia managed a mischievous grin. 'On a Brittany ferry. In the channel.'

'Good, good. On holiday, is he?'

'Actually no. A passenger has been stabbed. It's a murder enquiry.'

'But a Brittany ferry? Portsmouth? Bit out of our jurisdiction surely?'

Alicia's grin creased even further. The Chief had never seen her so amused. 'It's not where the man was killed. It's who the man is. Prepare yourself for a shock!'

The storm had died away. The sea was unnaturally calm. It reflected the gold of the rising sun as if in a mirror of blue, stretching out in all directions as far as the eye could see. As Jenny walked into the cabin, she was rendered breathless by the beauty of the view, filling the floor to ceiling windows with gilded light. Ken, too, was dumbstruck for a moment – in his case by the luxury of the cabin. It was as good as those he'd seen on cruise ships: a spacious stateroom, with a large comfortable double bed; an ensuite bathroom; a large sofa; wide screen television. D.I Forbes noted his surprise. 'A commodore cabin. With a balcony. It's top of the range. They're not all like this!' And with that, they focused their attention on the bed and what was lying on it.

The Hampshire pathologist, examining the body, wasn't one Ken knew. He looked like a schoolboy's impression of a mad scientist: white coat too small so that his wrists, protruding from the sleeves, looked unnaturally bony and long; grey hair unbrushed and sticking out from his head like an uneven mop. The crown of his head was bald, pink, and shiny. He had removed the victim's shirt and was examining the stab wound. It was an ugly gash in his back, close to the spine There was a lot of blood. The sheets were drenched in red. 'The cause of death is pretty obvious,' he intoned, without even turning round to see who had entered. 'It's a shallow wound but it's cut through an artery. It could have been the shock that rendered him unconscious. Then he just bled to death. To lose this amount of blood, he must have still been alive for at least ten minutes after the initial attack. The pain would have been severe. There is no sign of a struggle or of any movement after the stabbing, so it seems that, mercifully, he never regained consciousness.'

D.I.Forbes gestured toward the pathologist and then to the two officers who'd just joined the team. 'Professor Bradshaw. We're lucky to have him. He's the best there is.'

The professor waved this away. 'Take no notice. He's flattering me to make up for taking me across a rough sea, in a Force 8 gale, in a tiny motorboat. I've been spewing my guts up for hours!'

Forbes smiled. 'We had a lifeboat on standby in Poole. If the boat sank, there was a good chance they'd have reached us within what – ninety minutes!'

'By which time I'd have long drowned. And your esteemed colleagues?'

'Ah yes,' added Forbes. 'From Dorset. D.I. Kenneth Jones and Detective Sergeant Jenny Grace.'

The pathologist drew himself erect and took a long, shrewd look at the newcomers. Ken was surprised at how tall he was. At least six feet three with a thin and bony build. 'Jones, eh,' the professor mused. 'Heard some good things about you. From my counterpart in leafy Dorset. Sheila Peterson. You're friends, I think.'

Jenny's dark eyes sparkled as she turned to see the effect of this comment on her boss. Ken, in his turn, blushed furiously. 'I...I,' he stammered, 'value her expertise...A valued colleague!' Jenny suppressed a giggle. She knew very well that Ken and Sheila had a far from professional relationship and it had become very difficult for them both. Ken tried to change the subject to divert attention from his romantic entanglements. 'Can you give a time of death, professor?'

The elderly man sighed. 'Air conditioning. Bloody nuisance. Keeps everything cool. But judging by the clotting and the stiffness of the joints, roughly five hours ago.'

Ken turned to Forbes. 'Who found the body?'

'The cabin steward. He needed to take an order for breakfast and when there was no reply at the third attempt, he used his pass key to gain entry.'

'There's no sign of forced entry?'

'No. Either the killer had a key, or the victim welcomed him in.'

'Or her,' Jenny corrected.

Forbes, clearly annoyed at her interjection, swung round to the pathologist. 'Could it have been a woman? It looks as if the knife went in with some force.'

The elderly expert shrugged. 'Until I do a PM it's hard to say. If it's just gone through skin and tissue, it could have been a woman. If it's sliced through bone, it would indicate a great deal of strength.'

'And there's no sign of the weapon?' Ken mused.

'I suppose it could be at the bottom of the sea by now. But there could be fingerprints...DNA?'

'We'll have a scene of crime team all over this soon,' Forbes promised. 'But how did a knife get on board anyway?' He turned to the purser who had been cowering in a corner. 'Do you speak English?'

The Purser nodded dumbly. Jenny had travelled on French ferries. She had a high regard for the crew's linguistic skills. She cut in. 'All the crew have a working knowledge of English. They have far more British passengers than French!'

'Are there security checks before passengers board the ship – like at airports?' Ken demanded.

The Purser looked confused for a moment then shook his head. 'Sometimes...random searches of cars. All lorries are checked.'

'But people? Are they scanned? For weapons?'

'What would be the point?'

Ken pressed on: 'The point would be that no-one would be able to bring a knife on board!' And he gestured pointedly at the wound in the back of the unfortunate victim.

'But the cars are full. Full of *les choses* – things, *oui?* It would take days to empty and check them all! *Impossible!*'

Forbes nodded. 'And when you see the restaurants, you'll see there are knives everywhere. Already on board. The ship works on trust. It's the only way they can run and keep to any sort of meaningful schedule. There's never been any trouble before. That right?'

The Purser nodded, smiling, glad that someone, at least, understood.

Jenny was worried about the captain and her crew members. There was nothing she could do in the cabin. She wanted to be useful rather than stand there like a spare part. 'I'll check on the hostage situation, shall I?'

Ken turned and nodded. 'Someone needs to go with you.' None of the Hampshire men seemed interested, Facing up to a gaggle of angry French *routiers* wasn't their idea of fun. The purser, however, was glad of an excuse to escape from the smell of blood.

'I will accompany you, *madame!*' he exclaimed gallantly. Jenny looked at him properly for the first time. He was smart in his blue uniform and black, highly polished shoes. He had that dark complexion that was natural to Frenchmen from the south the country. A good head of hair. She almost corrected him, she was a *mademoiselle,* but decided it really didn't matter. She wasn't that interested.

A loud dingdong from downstairs forced Olivia to

pause her make-up. It was the maid's morning off. She had to head down to answer the door. She walked past her husband's dressing room on the way to the stairs. Her lip curled with disapproval. So untidy. Husbands were like small children to her. Messy, often hard to understand and generally annoying. But unlike children, who eventually moved out, husbands tended to cling on. She had a son from her previous marriage, Jason, and that meant she had two children to contend with – or at least it seemed like that. There were constant arguments between them. Jason could do nothing right, it seemed. David criticised his friends; the way he dressed; his lack of ambition; his poor record at school; and his reluctance to join the business and graft – to name just a few areas of dissent. She found herself torn between the two of them. These periods when David was away on business were blissful days of calm.

But the doorbell rang again. She waved her fingers in the air, her hands like two bright pink butterflies, to dry her nail varnish. It was eight in the morning! Who could be calling this soon? Her stomach knotted as she glanced through the hall window and saw a police car on the drive.

Her hand shaking slightly, she opened the door a few centimetres. Two uniformed figures greeted her by respectfully removing their caps. The female officer spoke first. 'Mrs. Leverson?'

'Yes.'

'Can we come in, please?'

She looked blankly at them. The male officer cut in. 'I'm afraid we have some bad news for you…' They didn't wait for a response. Instead, they pushed past her into the elegant hall, with its beautiful damask curtains and lightly flocked wallpaper that cost more for one roll than they earned in a week. Olivia's eyes darted anxiously to their boots, but the two officers failed to register her dismay and tramped across her deep white carpet. PC Bradley moved towards the drawing room, with a curt nod to Jes, his colleague. He addressed Olivia in what he thought was a tone full of regret. 'You'll need a cuppa tea, love. You'd better make one, Jessy!'

The policewoman gave a resigned sigh and wandered toward the rear of the hall and, she hoped, the kitchen. Bradley pointed to one of the deep leather armchairs. 'You'll need to sit down, love. It's goin' to be a bit of a shock!' As she collapsed into the chair her robe opened slightly, exposing her legs high above the knee before she tugged the silk fabric back in place. Bradley switched on his bodycam, surreptitiously. She was, he thought, quite a looker. His mind drifted back to a woman in Bridport years ago, who had fallen into his arms when he broke the bad news to her. She had needed a lot of comforting, he remembered with a smirk. It had taken several visits, on his own, to meet her needs. In bed, mostly. In his mind, this had been the high point of his career. But this bird – God she was fit. He'd give her TLC all right – given half a chance. If it didn't work out, though, the camera footage would be worth watching.

Jenny had to hurry to keep up with the purser. He seemed eager to put as much distance as possible between himself and the crime scene. She walked past a reception desk, beyond spacious gift shops and signs to the cinemas, into the huge self-service restaurant. Here groups of people were sitting, looking bored and miserable. They had expected to be in Portsmouth by now and instead were still at sea, nursing the remains of unplanned breakfasts. The purser stopped abruptly and pointed to the buffet bar, which still had a few croissants and a handful of fried eggs – but little else. 'We must get to port soon. We cannot feed so many thousand people – how do you say? – indefinitely!'

Jenny nodded. She tried to reassure him, but to be honest had little idea what the Hampshire force had in mind. 'We'll do our best. There are procedures…we have to go through…especially when there is a fatality…'

The purser shrugged. *'Je comprend,* but maybe one of your officers could speak to the passengers, no?

Explain? *C'est possible?'*

Jenny nodded, but she wasn't sure if this could be done or who could do it. She wondered if D.I. Forbes was aware of how bad the situation on board was getting. She felt suddenly helpless. She was a woman and not all male officers gave female officers the respect they deserve. She was the most junior there. And she was black. If Ken had been in charge, things would be different. She trusted him and knew that he respected her. But this was an odd situation. It wasn't clear why they were there or what role they were meant to fill. They'd been flown in without any preparation. Was this a joint operation – or were they just tagging along because the victim was a leading citizen of their county? But she had no more time to ponder on this. They were ushered through a door into what she realised was the part of the restaurant reserved for long distance lorry drivers. And what she saw stunned her.

The diminutive captain was standing in front of the two female members of her crew who had been taken hostage. She was between them and the lorry drivers. She was poised with her back arched and her legs slightly apart, in a position of authority. She wagged an imperious finger at the assembled men - all taller and stockier than her. A stream of French invective poured from her throat and the men began to look abashed and sorry for themselves. Jenny understood nothing of what was being said, but had no problem getting the gist of it.

One of the drivers, a short man with bristly hair in a spiky cut that made his round head look like the stub of a worn-out toilet brush, plucked up the courage to put their case to the captain. There was a hint of a whine in his tone. Clearly, he was as overawed by her anger as the rest of the group. Jenny couldn't understand a word that was said, but gathered that he was explaining the logistical difficulties any further delay would bring. His tone suggested that he didn't hold out much hope that the captain would take their concerns seriously. His friends nodded as he spoke, grunted their agreement, but were by now too cowed to add their voices to his. His intervention brought the captain to an even higher level of invective. She dismissed their concerns with a grand wave of an arm and then walked to the door, signalling to the hostages to exit through it to freedom. The two women, Jenny now worked out that they were both cashiers from the restaurant, slid gratefully out, with a multitude of '*Mercis*' to their new hero, the captain. Not one of the drivers moved to prevent their escape. She crossed her arms below her ample bosom and stared them out.

Jenny took a deep breath. She had little knowledge of their language, but felt obliged to lend her support. Maybe she could explain to the lorry drivers the reason for the delay – it was necessary, a protocol when murder was suspected – and perhaps the captain would translate the words for her. She felt that any assistance she could give would be at best slight, but she felt a duty to try. As she stepped forward, her heart pounding, Forbes barged through the door.

He'd been in touch with command headquarters. It would be too difficult to fly a SOC team out to the ferry. They were waiting for them in port. The passengers in nearby cabins had all been interviewed and had heard nothing. The cabin steward had been eliminated from their enquiries. All available CCTV footage from the cameras on board had been confiscated for scrutiny back at base. And the scenes at the ferry terminal were turning nasty. Thousands of would-be passengers were in danger of missing part of their holiday or of missing urgent business appointments. And it seemed that the entire French lorry fleet had been brought to a standstill. There were threats of blockades. And in France, threats of blockade were taken very seriously indeed. There was nothing else for it. The ship had to pick up speed and hurry to dock. Detective Inspector Forbes gave the news to the captain, who seemed, oddly, slightly disappointed as she waited in the doorway. It was as if she rather enjoyed holding her own against forty or more burly Frenchmen. But the news was greeted with a cheer by the men, who immediately began to pick up their belongings, ready to return to the safety of their cabs. But In order to leave, they had to file past the captain. Jenny was amused to see how their demeanour had changed. They bowed their heads and thanked her politely – like naughty boys apologising to their mother for their bad behaviour.

Olivia sat alone in her multi-million-pound property in the beautiful countryside round Fifehead Magdalen in Dorset. From the window seat in the master bedroom, she gazed out across the deer park. The officers had asked if there was someone they could contact – a friend, a relative – but she had said no. She wanted some time alone to take it all in. She felt numb and tired. So this was it. David was gone.

Out of sight of Olivia, half a kilometre away, a hungry fox poked his nose from his burrow. He could see the house in the distance, but the tragedy within meant nothing. He was planning his own killing - concentrating on the need to get food for his cubs. It was best to go hunting at night, but the farmer's chickens were locked up then, safe from predators. His cubs began to mew deep in their lair, complaining of hunger. He edged out into the sunlight, every sense on high alert. If he could avoid the traps, a juicy chicken would be their supper tonight. Between the fox and the chicken range, two stags were sizing up to each other. The younger felt ready to assume leadership of the herd – and rights over the females. A short charge and antlers were locked. The older stag, more experienced, twisted his head sharply and the younger male cried out in pain. The battle was over. For now.

Oblivious to the dramas all around her, Olivia sighed and got to her feet. She walked through the top floor of the house. Bedrooms, bathrooms, dressing rooms. Too many to count. All this, she mused, would soon be hers alone. David had not made a will: in his mid-forties he still had many years ahead of him. There would be time enough, he had thought, for legal niceties in time to come. Everything, she assumed, would come to her as his legal spouse. She had only just lost him, not yet identified the body, but couldn't help herself. She was planning her future. No need now to discuss colour schemes or to argue over curtain fabrics. From now she was in sole charge. It came as a surprise: a disconcerting feeling.

She hadn't realised until that moment how useful it had been to sound out her ideas with someone. If things didn't turn out right, all the blame would not fall on her. He had been a sounding board, if sometimes an annoying one. Slowly she stepped down the grand, curving staircase. She would pour herself a G and T. And wait for her son to return home. They would have to face the world alone.

This is what she had dreamt of for months. But the suddenness of it all was still a shock. The silence in the house began to torment her. To her surprise, the house felt unbearably empty and she felt achingly alone...

The huge ship purred into life and the bow swung towards the distant land, which could now be seen as a vague thin smudge along the horizon. Jenny pushed her way through the crowds of relieved passengers piling up at the stairwells that led down to the car decks. The doors to the lower sections of the ship were still locked. They wouldn't be opened until the ship was safely docked at the Portsmouth ferry port. She headed for the a la carte restaurant, happy to meet up with Ken; begin to discuss what had happened; and, perhaps, form an initial plan of how to proceed.

This eating venue was far superior to the self service one she had been in earlier. It was decorated in a manner that reminded her of the work of Rennie Mackintosh: stylish columns and very tasteful décor suggested this catered to passengers prepared to pay a little extra for the best. Maybe a lot extra, she thought. Waiters were already setting the tables for the return journey. White damask cotton tablecloths, wine glasses, silver cutlery. A tiny vase on each table held a single orchid. The menus were covered in dark leather. The bottles of wine left on view to tempt the discerning looked expensive. She saw Ken through the glass doors at the far end of the huge room. He was standing at the front of the ship, staring towards the distant land. Getting a breath of fresh air, she thought. She moved to join him.

She didn't need to speak. As soon as she was alongside him, he greeted her. 'Hi Jenny. How was it with the hostages?'

'How did you know it was me? It could have been the knifeman, looking for another victim!'

'If it was, he was wearing your perfume!' he said, with a smile.

'I'm flattered that you notice.'

'We've been together a long time. Of course I remember.'

Yes, thought Jenny. A long time. But even though she had to suppress her feelings for this man she so admired, she wanted nothing more than to remain an essential part of his team. She pushed her personal feelings to one side. This was business. 'The hostages weren't thrown overboard, if that's what you were fearing, boss. The captain was amazing. All those men were scared shitless of her. You should have seen it!'

'I can imagine! The ACC has the same effect on me!'

'She'd never sack you! She knows how good you are! And once you've been on telly, well...'

Ken smiled ruefully. 'That won't endear her to me! She hates the whole idea of it. So do I, if I'm honest!'

'I know what you mean. It's not a bit of me, either, being interviewed and all. But you'll be great. Star quality, that's you!'

Ken shook his head, but, before he could reply, his phone rang. Jenny moved back, but he stopped her. 'It's all right – just a text.' But then Jenny saw his face fall.

'Bad news?' Jenny asked. 'Is it HQ?'

Ken smiled and shook his head. 'Worse than that! Sheila!'

'Oh.' Jenny tried to believe that her dislike for Sheila, her certainty that she was the wrong life-partner for her boss, was entirely objective. She thought she knew him better than the pathologist ever would. The way Sheila had hurt him was unforgiveable. The way she'd rejected him for a man so much older, so much less handsome...she could go on and on. She was glad it was over. Surely it was. Ken was far too sensible to get involved again. In her opinion, he'd had a lucky escape! She couldn't help her disapproval showing on her face as she continued: 'I'll give you a minute.' And she walked away.

Ken hardly noticed as he stared at the message

on his screen. Sheila was suggesting that they meet at a neutral venue – in other words, not her apartment – to have a heart to heart. To finally sort out how they wanted this to end. Should they have one more go at establishing a relationship together, or call it off for good? Ken was torn. He knew something had to be done, but what? It was certain that he found Sheila extremely attractive – who wouldn't? – but was she right for him? Or him for her? And if not, if he had serious doubts, wouldn't it be better to call it off now? Refuse to meet? Wasn't it asking for trouble to agree to a meal together? On the other hand, had he really misjudged her, as a friend had said? The way she had treated him over her affair with Harold, her boss: had he judged her too harshly? Had he only thought of himself and not considered her feelings? It was not without a sense of foreboding that he a tapped a thumbs up emoji into his phone and wrote that he would contact her when he was back on land to arrange a time and place. The reply came swiftly. Just an emoji of two red lips blowing a kiss. He blushed and deleted it before Jenny could see it.

He walked over to where she was standing, at the rail, staring over the calm sea to the blue-grey strip of land that grew larger every second. They could just make out the Emirates Tower – the emblem of Portsmouth. As the cool wind blew through his thick head of hair, hardly disturbing the tight knot of black curls that adorned Jenny, he tried to clear his mind of his personal problems and concentrate on the next stage of the investigation.

'There's nothing more we can do until we land.'

Jenny nodded in agreement. 'I've never felt more bloody useless. This is Hampshire's baby really. We're just here as a courtesy.'

Ken nodded glumly. 'The SOC team will go over the cabin with a fine toothcomb. If they can find fingerprints and DNA it'll help. Until then, we have two and a half thousand suspects and no way of processing them all.'

Jenny turned and stared at the front of the huge white ship which was now cruising steadily towards its berth. 'Spooky to think that we're sailing with a killer on board!'

'And not a clue who it is,' Ken agreed. 'If they had CCTV in the corridors, it would help, but it's only in the main lounges. We'll go through frame by frame. It may show someone acting suspiciously – watching the victim or following him…but I don't hold out much hope.'

'Hours of work for someone,' Jenny agreed. 'I'm just glad it's not on our patch. We're busy enough without wasting hours watching useless video.'

'We'll have to help with the interviews though. And it'll be messy. It means catching up with all the passengers to find out where they were last night and what they saw.'

Jenny gave him a startled glance. 'All of them! It'll take weeks! We'll need help!'

Ken nodded. 'Let's track down Forbes and check what he's planned.'

The two of them walked back into the restaurant. Jenny felt her stomach rumble and realised she hadn't eaten for quite a while. Some breakfast would be nice. Happily, she spotted the Hampshire squad at a table not far away. As they walked towards them, Forbes waved. 'Sit yourselves down. We've managed to scrounge a few croissants. Help yourselves!'

More than a few. A plate was piled high with pastries and there were small packs of marmalade, strawberry jam and apricot conserve to pick from. She picked up two, desperate for food. For the last eleven months, since starting her diet, she'd avoided pastries. At a funeral, a year ago, she had been acutely embarrassed at how tight her uniform had become. She'd felt podgy and unattractive. It was a formal occasion, the internment of a murder victim in Bishop Farthing, and so uniforms were a must. Ken had attended too. He hadn't seemed to notice her figure, but she had felt so self-conscious and unattractive that she'd determined to sort herself out. A strict regime had followed. As a result, she was almost two stone lighter. Now, she felt much better about herself. Though Ken didn't seem to notice.

Ken finished one croissant and was helping himself to freshly brewed coffee. The pastries were delicious – the best he'd ever tasted – still warm from the oven. He gave the French a mental tick for their patisseries. He swallowed hard and then turned to D.I. Forbes. 'We were wondering how you're planning to proceed. When we dock. About interviewing the passengers!'

Forbes nodded, acknowledging the problem. 'I've called in all the manpower we can muster. About twenty uniforms will meet us at Arrivals. Hopefully they've organised desks and chairs. As the cars reach customs, we'll separate out those who live a distance away, using info from passports and driving licences. These we'll direct to an area where we can process them. The ones who live more local, we'll let them go, but tell them we'll be contacting them in the next couple of days so they can make a statement. It's the only way we can handle so many. We can't do them all at once. Impossible.'

Ken nodded in agreement. 'And the local ones – we divide them up?'

Forbes nodded. 'If you don't mind. We'll clear it with your Chief, of course. Hopefully not too many from Dorset, but we can't be sure yet.' Ken signalled agreement. 'That leaves the crew. But I can't see that it was a done by any of them. There's no possible motive.'

Ken's brow was furrowed with thought. 'No. Everything suggests this was a premeditated attack. Someone brought a knife on board. Took it to the cabin. Could have thrown it overboard?'

Forbes agreed. 'This wasn't a sudden thing. Someone angry over something that had been said or a lover's tiff. It was planned in advance. Not a crew member then.'

'So what was the motive? Once we find that, we've got the killer.' Ken dunked his Danish pastry into his coffee cup and then chewed on it. 'Someone's going to benefit from the death. Or he had a dangerous enemy. Someone who bore a grudge. A business partner?'

Forbes agreed. Ken continued, 'I assume his family would benefit from his death. Inherit his estate. And he was worth a fortune. Was anyone related to him on the passenger list?'

Forbes shook his head. 'He was travelling alone. A business trip. No-one from his immediate family on board.'

The ship gave a judder. They looked up in surprise. While they'd been talking, they'd reached port. Below them, the vessel was being secured to the dockside before the giant doors could be opened and the first vehicles could disembark.

'Are you happy for us to interview the close

family?' Ken queried. 'We'll need to eliminate them, even if they weren't actually on board.'

Forbes nodded. 'Probably a formality, but it needs to be done. They'll gain the most, after all. Check them out and then get back in touch?'

'Will do.' Ken smiled at Jenny. 'My sergeant is a wonder at dealing with ladies in distress. She'll be invaluable.' Jenny gave a half smile in return. It sounded like a compliment. But she'd rather be valued for her intellect and detective skills than for her ability to soothe weeping women. 'Do you want us to help out with the interviews as the passengers leave the ship?'

Forbes thought for a moment and then shook his head. 'It's just routine. You'll be more use to me checking out the family. I know how sharp you are. I'll value your opinion.'

Ken couldn't help but be flattered. 'I'll do my best. Won't let you down!'

And moments later Ken and Jenny were back outside, enjoying the open air on the front of the ship, looking in amazement at the long rows of cars and lorries waiting for their turn to board. 'It doesn't look possible, does it?' Jenny mused. 'How do they fit them all in?' Ken shook his head. He didn't know. But he was puzzling why someone would plan to commit a murder on an enormous cross channel ferry. What was the advantage? Could it be that he knew it would be impossible for the police to hold the vessel indefinitely? That they would have to let it dock so he could escape? If so, they were dealing with a cunning killer. And that could make this investigation all the harder.

Jenny broke in on his thoughts. 'When is your interview? On the telly? It must be soon!'

Ken's expression was grim. 'God. I'd forgotten about it. Day after tomorrow.'

'Don't worry!' She looked at her handsome boss: tall, well built, blue eyed, lightly tanned face. She had no doubt he'd come over well on the box. But Ken was far from sure. He blamed Wendy, the crime reporter from the local rag for this. He had no ambition to be a media personality. And he couldn't imagine any good coming of it.

Olivia poured herself a gin, choosing one with a hint of berries, delightfully pink as it left the bottle. Three ice cubes tinkled into the glass, then a slice of fresh lemon, before she topped it up with tonic. She sipped it slowly, relishing the flavour and the kick of the alcohol. Waving to the maid to clear up the remains of the lemon, she walked through to the drawing room. Her son was home. They'd had a few quiet moments together, hugging and reflecting on what had happened and what was to come. Now it was time to contact the family solicitors. She picked up her phone and touched the screen to bring it to life.

A woman's voice answered. A very refined accent. She sounded as if she'd been to Roedean and emerged with a GCSE in needlework and little else. 'Delware and Conroy.'

'I need to speak to Mr Forbingham.'

'I'm afraid he's very busy. May I take your name and number? I'm sure he'll call you when he's free.'

Olivia was having none of that. 'Young woman. I am Olivia Leverson, of Magdalen Hall.'

Silence. Then: 'I'm sorry, madam. If you'll just give me a moment...'

It's amazing the doors that the mention of money can open. A few moments of crackle on the line, then a rather squeaky man's voice came tinnily through the speaker: 'Mrs Leverson! How lovely to hear from you! I do apologise for the short delay!' Then, obsequiously, 'How are you? And your delightful family?'

Olivia came straight to the point. She needed to inform him immediately that her delightful family was now one short and discover the legal and financial implications of her loss. 'Sad news, I'm afraid, Geoffrey. The police called this morning. My husband is dead.'

'Dead! Good God! Was it his heart? Such a shock! Dear lady! Whatever we can do... Our firm is at your disposal. What a tragedy. So young! Or an accident? Are you with him now?'

'Not exactly. He's still on the ferry as far as I know. He's been stabbed! I'll have to go and identify him of course. I'm not sure when.'

Gasps. 'A knife? A ferry? Am I hearing aright? Hard to believe…'

Olivia was not concerned about the problems her solicitor was having with credibility. There were more urgent matters to discuss. 'Correct me if I'm wrong, Geoffrey, but I don't believe that David had got round to making a will?'

'Indeed, indeed, dear lady.' It was time to cover himself. This may be leading to a complaint. 'I spoke to him many times on the subject. There will be notes of our conversations. An unfortunate oversight – on his part. He was firmly of the opinion that there was no need at this stage – only in his late forties – many years ahead of him…'

'Yes, yes. But I need to think of my future security. For me and my son. In cases like this, would there be a problem with inheritance? I had to sign, I remember, a pre-nuptial agreement…'

'No, dear lady! Dear lady, no! You can rest assured on that! The agreement only comes into force in the event of a divorce! And as for the will, our firm will look after everything for you! In the case of a husband dying intestate, all his property automatically goes to his next of kin – in this case, his good wife!'

'So we'll be financially secure? Nothing can go wrong? You understand I am only, in this time of grief, thinking of my son.'

'Of course. I completely understand.' There was a pause as he mentally scanned every legal clause, every previous case, spanning hundreds of years. 'The only circumstance in which a wife would not be allowed to inherit, is if she had actually killed her husband!'

A moment of shock. 'Well. That hardly applies in this case!'

'Dear lady, no! I only gave it as the most extreme example! It would be seen as benefiting from the proceeds of a crime. But this could not apply to you! I only mentioned it so that you had the whole picture. Totally irrelevant in your case!'

'Bloody right! Well, that's settled. Can you begin the legal work? Begin to transfer assets?'

'So soon? I mean, of course, my dear. We'll begin to draw up a list of his assets today. Please accept, on my behalf and on behalf of the firm, our sincere condolences! Such a shock! Such a terrible loss!' And then, an afterthought: 'I hope that we will be able to continue to look after all your legal and financial affairs long into the future?'

''I'm sure.' She ended the call. Olivia looked round at the house. Through the tall windows she glimpsed just a small section of her estate. Her hand stroked the cabinet that held all the most recent financial statements – the shareholdings, the off-shore accounts, the insurance policies. Yes, she was a widow. She would miss David in many ways. But there were certainly advantages in her new status. Blinking back a tear, she managed just the hint of a smile.

Whoever declared that money can't buy you happiness, she thought, was going to the wrong shops!

She went back to her phone and phoned Nikki's husband. It was time to let Michael know the news...

Ken and Jenny left the ship by the passenger gangway, mingling with all the men, women and children who had not joined the ship by car. All were carrying heavy bags or sported large backpacks, so they got bumped into regularly as they descended. Most were in a hurry – understandable after the long delay they'd experienced. A young man with a shock of blonde hair – no more than eighteen, almost knocked Jenny over. 'Sorry...' he mumbled. Jenny smiled, her white teeth brilliant against her dark skin.

'It's okay. In a hurry to meet someone?' The youth nodded and rushed on. Jenny could not help staring at the faces around her and wondering if one of them could be the murderer. It made a chill run down her spine. She knew it was unlikely to be the grim-faced gentleman with the scar across his face and rough stubble round his chin. She had enough experience of hardened villains to know that they rarely matched any traditional stereotype. The criminal was more likely to be someone you would pass on the street and hardly notice. Someone clean shaven and respectably dressed. Maybe the short man smelling strongly of aftershave who was pressing up against her in the queue. She tried to pull away from him and snuggle up closer to Ken – the only person in the whole crowd she could be sure of!

When they reached ground level, they didn't board the crowded bus that took foot passengers to the terminal building to be processed. A patrol car was waiting for them with a friendly-faced traffic officer. 'Good morning, sir, ma'am. I've been sent to take you to your car.' A nice courtesy on the part of Hampshire, Ken thought, although they were more than capable of walking the short distance themselves. Things looked very different, in the morning sunlight, from last night, when it was pitch black, raining heavily and the area was lit by the landing lights of the police helicopter. He smiled. England looked good this morning. It was great to be back on dry land.

As they drove past the giant doors on the bow of the ferry, open to allow the first vehicles to leave, they saw three dark blue police vans, their blue lights flashing, waiting to enter. This was the SOC team, ready to go over the cabin where the murder had taken place. They would dust for fingerprints, photograph everything and search for evidence of DNA. Police procedure had come so far in the last twenty years that cold cases, old crimes that had lain unsolved for years, could now be solved. DNA traces could be sampled using advanced technology and a criminal who had thought himself safe from prosecution would suddenly feel the heavy hand of the law on his shoulder. Ken sighed. He just hoped that the SOC team would uncover some damning evidence and this case could be solved quickly and neatly.

Ken's car was far from the queues of those waiting to board. They were soon driving up to passport control. Jenny showed her police ID and they were waved through. She noted how the others were being redirected to the interview area, where a large marquee was awaiting them, staffed by as many officers as Hampshire could spare. She couldn't help wondering how long they'd be delayed. It was not the end to their trip abroad they could ever have expected. Ken concentrated on his driving as he steered them through the traffic lights system and onto the dual carriageway of the M275. Within minutes they were cruising smoothly along the M27 back towards their home county of Dorset. As the houses faded from view and the open countryside of the New Forest came into view, he relaxed and asked, 'What do you want to do, Jen? We need to call at Magdalen Hall and interview the family. We've been up all night, though. Do you need a break first? To freshen up?'

'Do I! I need a shower, at least.'

'Me too. And a change of clothes. I could get one of the team to set up a meeting this evening at the Hall. That would give us a few hours break.'

'That'd be great. My place is near here. We could stop there, have a shower, you could crash out on the sofa. If you're anything like me, you need some shut eye.'

What she said made sense. Her flat was in Poole. His two-bedroom terrace home was in Blandford. There was no good reason to turn her suggestion down. He couldn't help but feel a pang of anxiety about the plan, but, tired and needing rest, he hadn't the energy to think up an excuse to get out of it. Instead, he nodded and Jenny, comfortable next to him, felt pleased that they'd be relaxing together. Then she, too, was slightly worried. What state was her home in? She hadn't tidied it the day before, never expecting to entertain her boss there. When had she last done any dusting? And what about the washing up – had she cleared it away before leaving? And the bathroom. She blushed hotly. She must be sure that she went straight there – before Ken! She'd left underwear drying over the bath…

Alicia was surprised to get a call so early for a meeting with her boss. The Chief Inspector did not normally see anyone until halfway through the morning. It was well known amongst his closest colleagues that he spent the first two hours every day performing a detailed analysis of the financial pages of the national press. He had invested all his wife's inheritance – which was substantial – in stocks and shares. He enjoyed seeing his wealth expand. But if prices fell, he was intolerable for the rest of the day. Alicia checked the FTSE index on her phone as she walked down the corridor. Up ten points. She sighed with relief. He should be in a good mood.

She entered the outer office and gave her best imitation of a smile at Jane, his loyal secretary and PA. Jane was about five feet four, slim, with short auburn hair and eyes that seemed slightly too large for her face. It gave her an attractive, doe eyed look that Alicia rather liked. There was a lot about Jane that she liked. Her efficiency, her loyalty, her small breasts… She had made some effort to ingratiate herself with Jane. She'd even sent her a card last Christmas – an unusual honour. Alicia didn't believe in Christmas cards. Just commercial nonsense. Another attempt to get money from people, by convincing them that they should buy cheap cards and expensive stamps, and then send them to people they rarely met and didn't like. She had even given Jane her personal telephone number – in case anyone needed to contact her urgently out of hours. This was unnecessary, as she always had a police phone with her. She hoped that Jane would take the hint and understand that she was interested, but nothing had transpired. Alicia had decided that the many rumours must be true. Jane and the Chief must have something going together. It would explain Jane's total dedication to her role and her employer. Alicia tried the smile again. There was always hope, after all.

Jane did not appear to notice. 'He's expecting you. He said you're to go straight through.'

Alicia did as she was bid. A cursory knock and then she pushed the door open. The Chief looked up from the pink pages of the Financial Times and nodded to her. 'Ah Alicia, Thanks for coming so promptly! I was just...err...' He folded the paper and pushed it to one side. 'Just checking on the latest crime statistics.'

'Grim, aren't they?' Alicia decided to go along with this bending of the truth.

'Yes indeed.' The Chief settled back in his large

leather chair. 'There are villains amongst us, more's the pity.'

Alicia treated her Chief with respect because he was her senior officer. But there it stopped. He was typical, she thought, of men who'd been promoted beyond their abilities. In truth, she had little admiration for men in any position. He seemed to her to be slow thinking and frankly rather stupid. She was certain that when she inherited his position her quick, decisive mind would run the force much more efficiently. In secret, she was monitoring his expense claims. Already there was enough evidence to bring a case. He was falsifying his claims to finance his gambles on the stock market. The only question was a strategic one. If she were the one to bring the old man down, would it adversely affect her chance of being promoted into his place? Yes, there are villains amongst us, she agreed. But she would expose this particular one in her own time.

'This terrible business on the ferry.' The Chief detested terrible businesses. He liked to keep Dorset free of violent crime. It was better for his reputation. 'Unbelievable! Stabbed in the back, I believe! What will they think of next?'

'Luckily it didn't happen on our patch, Chief. I think that Jones and his team will simply be there to assist the Hampshire force.'

'Indeed, indeed. But this is causing ripples in

high places.' Indeed, it was. The victim was an important – and very wealthy – member of the lodge. Many very senior masons had already been in touch to ask him how the investigation was going. And he didn't know. 'It would be best if this could be cleared up quickly. And the killer brought to justice, don't you know. What info have we got on the way things are going?'

Alicia knew better than to admit she had nothing. She put her hands together in a prayer posture, as if she had brought the Almighty alongside. 'Still very early days. But we're following a number of promising leads. We have the details of all the passengers and each one will be tracked to their homes and interviewed separately.' This sounded safe. She could relax. Or so she thought.

'All the passengers? How many were on board? Thirty? Forty?'

Alicia gulped. She hadn't realised how out of touch her boss was with modern travel. 'Rather more actually.'

'How many more?'

I understand,' she hesitated, but she saw no alternative than to come clean, 'the ship was carrying approximately two thousand four hundred passengers…'

'Two thousand four hundred? You're joking!'

No, she wasn't. 'And then there's the crew…'

'And they've been allowed off the ship? Allowed home? Escaped? So whoever did the murder is... just released back into the country?' The Chief was turning a rather nasty shade of puce. Alicia brightened. Was he about to have a stroke? This could be the opportunity she had been waiting for. But alas, he continued to breathe and was staring at her accusingly. It was time to move the blame elsewhere.

'Shocking. I know. I was equally astonished. But it's out of our hands, sir. Hampshire are firmly in charge.'

The Chief settled back into his chair, tutting loudly. But yes, he was somewhat mollified. Whatever came of it, no blame could possibly be assigned to them. And then there was this other rather odd case. He opened a deep drawer in his desk, conveniently close to his right knee. From it, he pulled a cut glass decanter containing an amber liquid. And a tumbler. He gave Alicia an enquiring raise of one eyebrow. 'No, sir – not for me.' He nodded. It was the reply he expected. His ACC was efficient and reliable, but lacked, it seemed to him, a certain worldliness. She was too straightlaced, too removed from the realities (and pleasures) of life to ever rise further. To reach his elevated position, a candidate needed to mix comfortably with councillors, government ministers, high society. No, she'd gone as far as she would ever go. He sighed. Still, she had her uses. A queer bird, though, he ruminated.

A long, pleasing sip of single malt lubricated his throat before he ventured: 'So, with Hampshire safely in charge, there's probably not a great deal for Jones and his team to do?' She nodded warily. 'In which case, there's another case he could follow up for me. And it's a damned odd one…!'

Ken's car pulled up at the apartment block that held Jenny's one bed flat. She enabled him to enter the underground parking with a press of her key fob. Then she surveyed the rows of spaces. Each owner had a single parking space. The architect had allocated three spaces for visitors. There were more than a hundred apartments. The visitor spaces were always going to be full, even if they weren't occupied by owners who had two cars and felt entitled to an extra space. It was as Jenny expected. All three were occupied. She pointed to a vacant space below a leaking pipe.

'Use that one! It belongs to Anne. She works till five, so she won't need it till then.'

Securely parked, they took the lift to the third floor. Jenny felt suddenly apprehensive. The last time he'd visited her flat, almost two years ago, they'd both been tipsy and they'd ended up sleeping together. It had meant a lot to her, but, it seemed, little to Ken. He hadn't even mentioned it since. This had hurt her more than she was prepared to admit, even to herself. She felt safe with Ken. She knew he wouldn't force himself on her. But it felt awkward, this second visit, for reasons she couldn't quite put her finger on. She shrugged mentally and put it all to the back of her mind as they exited the lift and walked to her door. Ken was silent, absorbed in thinking, not about the last time they staggered through this door together, but about the current case. And when he spoke, it was nothing that Jenny expected.

'If we're going to interview the widow this evening, we'll need some background. I'd better get the office to run a background check. And if only to eliminate her from the enquiry, find out about her financial situation. I'd guess she's in line to inherit a small fortune. This was probably done by someone who gains something from his death. It may be money. It could be revenge. Either way, the more we can find out the better.'

Jenny's mind flipped a somersault. Once she had refocused, she agreed. 'Sure boss. I'll call Nigel and get him to do a full check, including bank details. Do you think the wife could have done it?' She looked doubtful.

'It's not possible, is it?' Ken agreed. 'She wasn't on the ship. But the more we know, the firmer our position will be.'

They walked into Jenny's small but comfortable living area, which also contained a small kitchen. Jenny pointed to the sofa. 'Rest there – I'll make us a pot of tea.' No alcohol this time.

Ken collapsed into the colourful cushions – Jenny was a fan of bright red, blue and green, reminiscent of her family's Caribbean background – and by the time Jenny had boiled the water and dunked two tea bags into the mugs, he had fallen asleep. Jenny walked over, tea in hand, and gazed on her boss, fast asleep on her sofa. She smiled. It was the kind of loving smile a young mother might give as she gazes on the face of her sleeping toddler. She crept quietly to the bedroom, selected a dark blue blanket, and draped it carefully over him, resisting the temptation to place a gentle kiss on his cheek. Well, she thought, at least the problem of who would sleep on the bed is resolved.

But before she could allow herself to rest, there were calls to make. She didn't mind. Jenny felt useful and efficient as she asked Nigel, the team's tech guru, to check on the bank details that Ken had requested. It turned out that Hampshire had already sent a list of the passengers with Dorset addresses (or nearby) that had been allocated to their team. They'd sent a list of questions for the interviews, to ensure a consistent approach. But the office was in turmoil. There were over two hundred separate visits to organise and Hampshire, of course, wanted a quick turn round.

She told them that Ken would get straight onto it, hoping they couldn't hear the soft snoring coming from the sofa. Her duty done, Jenny at last laid down for some much-needed rest.

And it was this same pressure on resources that was troubling the Chief Constable. He shared his concerns with Alicia. 'There's this royal visit…'

'But it's very low key. Not official.'

'True. But the protection people are insisting that we check the whole fifty-acre estate the day before and keep officers on guard overnight to ensure total safety.' The royal couple were due to visit the queen's aunt. Only a courtesy call – a quick lunch engagement. They'd arrive by helicopter from Highgrove around noon, land at the aunt's estate near Wimborne, and be gone by three. It was, in the Chief's opinion, though patriotic and a devout royalist, a damn nuisance. Budgets were tight. There would be overtime to pay – night work was expensive, and he'd need armed officers, more than Dorset could call on from their own resources. The visit was a private one. Nobody would know it was happening. The precautions he had to take were, in his opinion, excessive.

Alicia offered a suggestion. 'Would it relieve the pressure on you if I went to greet the royal couple when they arrive?' There was a glint of excitement in her eyes. Yes, this would be a chance to raise her profile. She'd ensure photographs were taken. How splendid it would be - a picture of Alicia with the royal couple to decorate her desk! The Chief's expression was one of amazed horror.

'No. No – absolutely out of the question. No matter how inconvenient, it is the Chief Constable's duty to be on hand to welcome the king to the county. Onerous though it often is,' he lied. 'But it's bad timing, when we've got this request from Hampshire - the questioning of all the ferry passengers who live around Dorset. Do you think Jones' team can handle all that on their own?'

'We can put some uniform on it, but they'll have to pull their weight. It'll make a change for them, not to be arresting fellow officers!'

The Chief squirmed slightly but decided not to take the bait. 'And then there's this other business.'

'Another?' Alicia was annoyed. She didn't like it when the Chief was aware of something that she had missed.

'Yes. This farmer's wife in Tarrant Hinton. Mrs...' he consulted a scrap of paper; 'Harvey. Saw some aliens trying to steal her sheep. Frightened them off with a couple of bangs from her shotgun.'

'Aliens? They'd come across on the small boats?'

A moment of confusion. The Chief's brow

furrowed and then gradually cleared. 'No. Not aliens like foreigners. Good heavens no. No – ones that come on flying saucers.'

'You can't be serious, sir!'

'Absolutely. Klingons she called them.'

'Klingons?'

'Your guess is as good as mine. They're some kind of spaceman, apparently. Jane tells me they feature in a science fiction series very popular on the television.'

'But we're not taking this seriously, are we? Surely she's off her head!'

The Chief shook his head with the resignation of a man who long ago gave up hope of living in a world dominated by the sane. 'Normally, you're right. This would go straight into the pending file also known as the wastepaper bin. But our esteemed Home Secretary has a bee in her bonnet about police forces not taking minor crimes seriously. Minor burglaries, men having a quick flash in parks: it's all to be investigated. Even hopeless cases. It only needs some aggrieved citizen to complain to their MP that we didn't turn up in person to investigate and we'll have the Home Office on our backs.' He contemplated this, morosely. 'And, even worse, the press!'

Alicia nodded. The times when the police could just cherry pick the easiest crimes to investigate were, sadly, over. But she could turn this to her advantage. 'Jones' sergeant, Grace, could handle this. If anyone is equipped to tackle monsters from Mars, it's her. She's friends with a woman psychic. Used her in the body in the bluebell wood case. She's gullible enough to convince this farmer woman that we take her seriously.'

The Chief had no idea what Alicia was talking about. But this happened often, and the best strategy in these cases, he had long ago decided, was to say nothing and give the impression that he knew everything. He nodded his assent and ended the discussion. He was keen anyway to get back to his scrutiny of the financial pages. The FTSE index was rising, but slowly. He may need to readjust his portfolio. So science fiction was popular. was it? But which companies sold it?

Jenny's alarm woke her at three pm. It took her brain a few seconds to focus on what had happened. She crawled out of bed and contemplated the problem of getting from the bedroom to the bathroom. It meant crossing the living room. She was not accustomed to having anyone else in her flat, let alone a man. She checked in the mirror that the T shirt she was wearing protected her modesty. It did, just. She peeped through the door. Good. Ken was still asleep. She tiptoed to the bathroom and remembered to lock the door. Normally on her own, she wouldn't even close it. As quietly as she could, she used the toilet and showered. When she emerged, wrapped in a large towel, Ken was waking. He surveyed her through half closed eyes. 'You've lost weight!' he exclaimed.

Jenny had been this slim for weeks but was secretly pleased that he had noticed it at last. She twirled. 'Thanks! Do you approve?'

'Yep. You look good.' But he was turning toward the small kitchen area. 'Shall I make some coffee?'

'No need. I'll do that. You go and freshen up.' Jenny was still uncomfortable about having someone else sharing her space. She wasn't used to it. He'd be in her bathroom. Using her soap and towels. Her toilet. It was all rather odd. This was Ken and she loved and trusted him. But they were no longer lovers – if they ever had been. And though they were friends as well as colleagues, it wasn't the sort of relationship where they spent time in each other's homes. And beneath the towel she was naked. And it was beginning to slip. She grabbed the top and was relieved to see him turn away and disappear into the bathroom. She stood for a moment breathing steadily and deeply to compose herself. Then she filled the kettle and set it to boil before turning to the bedroom to dress. As she reached the door, the towel finally gave way. She turned to scoop it up and glanced towards the bathroom. The door was closed. She sighed with relief. Embarrassment had been avoided, she was pleased to say. Almost pleased. She shrugged and closed the door behind her as she walked to the wardrobe.

When she emerged, in a crisp white shirt and dark blue jeans that hugged her body in – she thought – quite a flattering way, Ken was in the kitchen area with a small towel wrapped round the lower part of his body. She liked the fuzz of dark hair on his chest and the toned muscles of his arms. He turned to her. 'I heard the kettle boiling, so I thought I'd make the coffee. It's only instant.'

She couldn't help noticing the small bulge at his crotch. She still remembered their one night together, when for a brief few moments she had held the part of him that the towel was concealing. Realising that she was blushing, she pushed him back towards the bathroom. 'Leave it to me. You go and get dressed. I've nothing for you, I'm afraid. You'll have to wear the same clothes you came in.

'No prob. Back in a mo.'

Deep breaths again. This was both a pleasure and a torture. The answer, she thought, was to busy herself to take her mind off the strangeness and possible awkwardness of this. She found half a baguette, butter and some Cheddar. Two plates, two knives and a couple of tomatoes. Not much, but she hadn't planned to be entertaining. When

Ken returned – now fully dressed – he sat down and began to eat, telling her how grateful he was, and she began at last to relax. She watched him chew on the bread (slightly stale, it was two days old) and wondered how he was feeling. Did this seem awkward or strange to him? There was no sign that it did. He seemed perfectly happy, two colleagues sharing a snack together. How she wished she had his self-confidence. But then was that the answer – was he so mentally strong that nothing fazed him or was it a lack of awareness of the feelings of others? A bit of both, she decided. But she still respected him. Essentially, he was a fine, honest man and there were not so many of them around.

An hour later they were on the road driving towards Fifehead Magdalen. They slowed to thirty as they made their way through Shillingstone. They passed a small supermarket at the end of the main street and began the climb into the countryside. The road was narrow and twisting. They turned right at Sturminster bridge and passed the small, thatched building that held the town's fascinating museum, and then sped out past the secondary school playing fields towards Tarrant Hinton. Again, they had to slow, and it got little better as they followed the bends in the road to Marnhull and on towards Todber Hall. They finally reached the sharp turn into a narrow country lane leading to Fifehead Magdalen.

The church, dedicated to Saint Magdalen, is unusual because it has a central turret. Passing the gate to the graveyard, they enjoyed the lines of thatched houses and the countryside they could glimpse between them. It was hardly a village – more a large hamlet. Eventually they reached Magdalen Hall, found themselves facing heavy iron gates, and both stared in surprise at the house. They expected a sixteenth century manor, white walls, exposed timbers and thatched roof. Instead, they gazed at a long twisting drive, neatly made from paving blocks, curving through neat lawns and flower beds – not full of cottage garden plants, but ornamental grasses, colourful sages and phormiums. And at the end of the long drive, glimpsed through the modern prairie planting, along with ornamental rills and ponds, was a very different house from the one they expected. It looked as if it had been lifted, glass and startlingly white concrete, from Beverley Hills and dropped into the Dorset countryside. Ken left the car and walked to the answerphone on a post near the gates.

'Inspector Jones and Sergeant Grace. We've an appointment with Mrs Leverson.'

Silence. Crackle. Then a woman's voice, with a trace of a foreign accent: 'She is expecting you.' A click and a whirr and the gates began to swing slowly open. Ken got back into the car, and they drove along the winding drive to park beside the short, wide flight of steps, in simulated white marble, that led up to the impressive front door. Jenny felt the whole house was so intimidating that they ought, perhaps, to have parked at the back. Another intercom bell to push. Ken was ready to bark his name yet again, but he was saved the trouble. There was a loud click and the door swung open to reveal the maid, in a tight black dress and a white apron. She didn't speak, but gestured to them to follow her across a deep white carpet to the entrance to what Ken assumed was the drawing room. Light flooded in through large windows, opening onto the extensive green lawns. Jenny was taken aback by the sheer opulence of the room. The furnishings were obviously very expensive – way beyond a police officer's salary. She consoled herself, as she gazed at the extravagant drapes and the gold and crystal chandeliers, by telling herself that there was far too much bling. But secretly she had to admit that she was a tiny bit jealous.

Olivia was draped elegantly along a light beige sofa, clearly distraught, dabbing at her eyes which seemed to shed tears not damp enough to blot her mascara. Too grief stricken to speak or rise, she waved them towards another sofa and a low table laid with fine bone-china teacups, a plate of fancy biscuits and a small Wedgwood vase with tiny sprigs of fresh flowers. The two officers, feeling slightly overawed by their surroundings, perched on the edge of the seat.

Jenny produced a notebook and a pencil. Ken drew in a breath and began: 'Mrs Leverson, can we begin by expressing our sincere condolences. We are so sorry for your terrible loss.'

This brought another bout of choking sobs and tears from the grief-stricken widow. 'Such a shock!' she sobbed. 'Such a wonderful man! Taken so soon!'

Jenny was worried that the woman was alone, in such a large house, with no-one to comfort her at such a difficult time. 'Is there anyone who can come to stay with you for a while?'

Olivia dabbed her eyes again. 'Thank you, dear. My son is with me. He is my comfort. My rock.' Jenny looked round. She couldn't see any sign of a child.

'Is he here? Is he a toddler?' Perhaps it was his time for a nap.

'No.' Another sniff. 'A teenager. He's from my first marriage.' Olivia was feeling the effects of prolonged condolences. All her friends had been in touch. Not because they had heard anything from the mainstream broadcasters. They were not regular listeners to the BBC or ITN news. Their hectic social lives meant that they'd never got into the habit of watching television at six or ten o'clock. And anyway, these programmes required you to continue watching for at least half an hour. And if you did, most of it was not a bit of them.

Easier and faster to dip into social media and pick out snippets of genuine interest and import: celebrity gossip, fashion news. And it was from Facebook that they had heard of David's tragic death. How they buzzed with excitement, like bees around a newly opened honey pot. Here was real drama that affected one of their own. Nikki had been the first to call. David and Nikki had been, well, close. Tears had gushed as she shared in Olivia's loss. Nikki was closely followed by more and more as the news spread across the narrow band of internet that was the cloud on which these women float. A real-life drama was being enacted around and amongst their own. They all wanted a role within it. But there is only so much condolence that one woman could take. And Olivia had reached that teary limit.

Jenny, genuinely concerned, pressed on: 'Is he home? Should we talk to him? Tell him how sorry we are? Tell him we'll do everything to find out who did this terrible thing?'

Olivia shook her head. It was a struggle for her to speak. 'No...no. leave him. He's at college. Won't be back for a while yet. He's coping. In his own way. It's hard for both of us.'

'Of course.' Jenny wasn't reassured. She wondered if this mother, in her current bewildered and desolate state, was truly able to judge the impact of the loss of father on the stepson. She turned to Ken for reassurance, but his mind was back on the case.

'Mrs Leverson, I know this may not seem to be the time, but we must proceed with our investigation. We're still waiting for a full forensic report, but it seems most likely that this was a premeditated attack. Someone planned to kill your husband. Now, think carefully. Can you think of anyone who had a grudge against him? Or anyone who would gain from his death?'

Olivia looked blank and then shook her head.

'Anyone he does business with? Anyone he has crossed recently? Did he mention anyone who was troubling him?'

Olivia dabbed at her eyes again. Now the mascara was beginning to run. She looked in despair at the black stains on the tissue. It was clear to Jenny that she wanted the interview to end. Olivia turned soulful eyes to Ken and then reached out, touching his hand. 'I'm sorry. We never talked about his work. He wanted this house, his home...' she swallowed a sob, 'to be a place where he could relax. Escape from the stress...'

Ken nodded and pressed her hand reassuringly. 'We'll leave you. But here's my card. If you think of anything – no matter how insignificant it may seem, then don't hesitate to get in touch. You never know. It may be the lead we need.' Olivia gave a sad smile and nodded. She took the card, folding her fingers around it. Jenny watched as the newly widowed woman turned her eyes on Ken.

Maybe Jenny was jumping to conclusions, but she suspected that Olivia might indeed call, whether she had information or not. Her mind turned to their last training session. The lecturer had told them of recent research that surprised them all. It seems that there are possibly as many female psychopaths as male. It had always been assumed that cold, ruthless killers are almost all men, like Ian Brady or Ted Bundy (an American serial killer who murdered dozens of women and girls in the seventies). The lecturer explained the difference between the two types. Male psychopaths are more likely to kill and with greater cruelty. Women, it seems, are more likely to achieve their ends by manipulating, deceiving or bullying their victims. And when the lecturer added flirtation to that list, Jenny was alarmed. The look that Olivia gave Ken worried her. But she shrugged it off. The woman was wealthy, sophisticated and grieving. She could hardly be a psychopath!

But as Ken drove them away from the house, he was not aware of any possible interest that Olivia might have in him. He had suddenly remembered Sheila and his promise to get in touch. And that was stress enough.

Back at Dorset CID, the rest of the team were mulling over the order that had just come from the ACC to go to Tarrant Hinton and investigate an attack by aliens. They found it difficult to keep their faces straight. This was too ridiculous to take seriously. Surely a uniform could go, if any response were required at all. Still, it was a giggle. A little light relief. They knew that Ken and Jenny were fully occupied with following up on the ferry killing, so it was decided that Sarah, one of the more junior members of the team, should phone the lady farmer, to assure her that the police were onto the case and take down a statement. The call was put on speaker phone. Nobody wanted to miss this.

Sarah dialled. The number rang for what seemed ages then a young male voice answered. 'Yeah? What?'

Sarah swallowed and looked round at the expectant faces of her colleagues. They had already covered twenty of the ferry interviews and were glad of this diversion. 'This is Dorset police. CID. Could I speak with Mrs Harvey?'

A pause. 'She's muckin' art.'

Sarah looked round for support. None came. 'Could you call her? Ask her to come to the phone? We need to speak with her!'

'I'll try; 'old on.'

A long silence followed. Sarah began to worry that the line had dropped. Then the sound of heavy wellington boots approaching the phone, squelch after squelch of wet mud and cow poo. A woman's voice.

'Yes?'

'Dorset police, Mrs Harvey. We're following up on your complaint about trespassers…'

'Abart time! You've tekken bloody long enough! They'll be long gone now. Flown off, they will!'

'Our apologies. The police forces are severely stressed at this time. We have multiple investigations in hand. But maybe you can give a description – of what you saw?'

'It wa last night. It wa dark. There were flashing lights. Spooky noises, like in space films. Like flying saucers make. I got a gun…' Nigel scrambled to the computer to check on gun licences. Did this woman have a licence for a shotgun? 'I went out wi' a torch. Shone it on 'em. Saw their faces!'

This was a stroke of luck. Sarah jumped in. 'That's really helpful, Mrs Harvey. How many were they?'

'Four of the bastards. I saw at least four!'

'Can you describe them? Their heights? Build? Hair colour? Skin colour? Facial features?'

'That's easy. They all looked same!'

'All the same? Their faces?'

'Yeh. Klingons. Ev'ry one of 'em. Evil looking bastards. With big ridges on their forreds. Easy to spot. Can't miss'em.'

It wasn't often that Sarah was struck dumb with astonishment – but this was one of those rare occasions. She looked round at the others, helpless for a moment. Some looked puzzled, some very amused. No-one offered help. They were enjoying this as light relief in what was normally a dull and monotonous job. Their roles were generally to back up the small detective team and rarely had a break from their computer screens.

Finally, Nigel broke the silence. 'She has a licence okay. You'd better go out there and see her.'

Sarah wasn't sure why. 'To look for clues? Like crop circles and scorch marks? They can't really be Klingons, can they? Would there be marks where their saucer landed?'

Trevor offered guidance, only half seriously. 'Not Klingons. I've seen them on Star Trek. They don't have saucers. They have warbirds. Armed to the teeth. And they have cloaking devices. They can disappear at will. And take care – they're mean bastards!'

Nigel shook his head and attempted to reassure her. 'No, don't worry, you're not going to find aliens. But this woman has a gun licence. You'll have to check her out. We're not supposed to give licences to mad people. And she sounds barmy!'

Totally unaware of the problems that the staff in his office were having with extraterrestrials, Ken, having dropped Jenny back at her flat, was plucking up courage to call Sheila. They hadn't met since the murder of a girl in the student accommodation block in Bournemouth. That was when she had mocked him for not recognising Jenny's strong feelings for him. It was a revelation that had complicated his life even further: yet another relationship that he now looked back on with guilt. It was ironic that Ken – who thought of himself as a protector of women – so often seemed to be hurting them. But at that moment Sheila was his greatest problem. He knew that he had strong feelings for her once. Did he still? Her insistence that he wait for her to end her affair with her boss – a much older man – before they could be together had hurt him deeply. And then she had allowed this man to move in with her – believing his cock and bull story about his wife finding out about their affair and throwing him out. He still felt fury at the way she had treated him. But was this smothering the true feelings he still had for her? He had been more attracted to her than to any other woman he had ever met. Did he still feel that pull? Or was he secretly afraid that she had ice in her heart and could dump him when it suited her as coldly as she'd rid herself of his rival?

He had promised to call her. With some

trepidation he touched her name on his phone. She answered immediately.

'Ken! I thought you'd forgotten me again!'

'Sorry Sheila. It's the first chance I've had to call. I'm caught up on a case.'

'I've heard about it. The body on the ferry. Bernie Bradshaw rang me from Portsmouth. No complications apparently. Just a single stab wound deep into the back. Bled to death. He'd been drinking before the attack. Enough alcohol in his system to make it difficult for him to fight off his attacker. It would have dulled the pain. Still, a nasty way to go.'

Ken was slightly put out that Sheila had information more up to date than his. 'He said that he knew you.'

'Bernie? Yes. He was one of the professors who lectured on scene of crime forensics. Very experienced and quite a charming old duffer in his way. No wonder you're busy. There are two and half thousand suspects, I've heard!'

'I don't have to interview them all. But you said we should meet up?'

'Yes.' Sheila sounded slightly guarded. 'What do you think?'

'Yes. We need to talk. Tonight?'

'Suits me. On neutral ground?' She laughed. 'Or your place. I've never seen where you live!'

'It's nowhere near as grand as yours. Just a starter home.' He made an optimistic calculation of how long it would take to make it clean and tidy before he could risk her seeing it. 'Could be there though. In about an hour.'

'I can make that. Are you hungry?'

'I haven't eaten yet. And you?'

'No.' Sheila considered the options. 'We could get a takeaway if that's easiest for you.'

It was. 'There's a good Chinese on the high street if you'd like that.'

A bright response. 'I love Chinese! Be there in about an hour. Text me the address!'

Ken did so, wondering what he'd let himself in for.

His home was moderately tidy and fairly clean. He spent relatively little time there. A quick glance round proved, to him at least, that no housework was required. He found a bottle of supermarket Sauvignon Blanc and put it in the fridge. He was sure Sheila drank more expensive wine, but it would have to do. He showered, then dug out the rumpled card menu from the Chinese takeaway. He considered ordering in advance, but wasn't sure what Sheila would like, so left it on the coffee table. He just had time to straighten the bedding – though he wasn't expecting that she would see it – when the doorbell rang. A last check round. The furnishings were basic. A sofa bought in a DFS sale; a coffee table and a TV/hi fi unit from Ikea; plain pale blue curtains from Primark. A minimum of ornaments (just a vase from his mum) and a light grey carpet that was already fitted when he moved in. It was all he needed. This was just a base, rather than a home. Somewhere to relax, sleep, make simple meals.

A year earlier, he would be very nervous, worrying over what Sheila would make of it. It was so different from her apartment, with its prime view of Bournemouth seafront and expensive furnishings – all bought with the help of an inheritance from her grandfather. But now he felt relaxed. He'd do his best to make his peace with Sheila and then move on. He smoothed the white tee shirt over his dark, slim line jeans and answered the door.

'Hi Ken.'

'Sheila. Come through.' She smiled and brushed past him, casting a critical eye over the interior. It was much as she expected. She knew Ken well enough to have expected nothing more than this. He was a man and, therefore, not a nest builder. This was the unassuming bachelor pad she had anticipated. Clean though. She gave him credit for that. To be honest, she would have been worried if he turned out to be designer freak. It would have meant that she had seriously underestimated him. Anyway, it was of little consequence. At that moment, it was not the quality of his furniture that was the main issue. It was the quality of their relationship – if they were to have one at all.

'Have a seat. I haven't ordered yet – I wasn't sure what you'd like.'

'Thanks. But I'd have gone along with anything you chose.' She was looking at him very directly. It slightly unnerved him. She passed the crumpled card with its long list of dishes and helpful numbers (and prices) back to him. 'Surprise me.'

Ken hadn't expected this. He scanned the multiplicity of choices and was unsure what to do. Then he saw the Chinese Feast for two. Three mains, three sides. It looked okay. He picked up the phone. 'You're sure?'

She nodded. 'Anything.'

He gave the order, his address and paid in advance by card. 'Should be here in twenty minutes. They're very reliable. How about a drink. A glass of white wine?'

She was watching his every move with the hint of a smile. He felt increasingly unsettled. Was she laughing at him? He felt more and more awkward. He half filled two glasses and passed one to her. She noted that the glass was clean. Another plus, she thought. 'Cheers.'

She settled back into the sofa, her skirt riding up a little as she did so. She wore a rich blue flared skirt that emphasised her narrow waist and the curve of her hips. A loose-fitting cashmere sweater was cut so that it left one of her shoulders bare. She raised her glass to her lips. Then: 'Sit down.' She patted the seat beside her. 'We need to talk.'

Ken was caught out. He had planned that they would eat the food first, before the awkward discussion, and then it would be easier just to say goodbye. Much more difficult if they broke up and then had to eat a meal together. And he hadn't planned to sit so close to her. It had been such a rush that he had never thought it through. In his mind he had remained standing, putting distance between them. But it would seem very strange now to refuse. He sat with about ten inches between them. It was the best he could do. He looked stiff and awkward, in sharp contrast to her apparent ease.

Sheila waited a second for him to speak before realising that she would have to break the silence if they were not to remain like two cold marble statues until the food arrived. 'I know you think I treated you badly. But I don't believe you understand what I intended. The problem I was facing. The fact that I just needed time to sort things out.'

Ken hated this. He didn't want to go over this ground again and again. Yes, she might have a point. Maybe he'd jumped to conclusions. But nothing she could say – no rationalising over the affair now – could take away the hurt he had felt. He shrugged. 'I'm sure it…wasn't easy for you either.'

Sheila's eyes narrowed. She was carefully judging the impact of her words on this man she respected, even loved, but who lacked the empathy to see things from her perspective. 'I'm not asking for sympathy. If you've decided it's over and the two of us can't work this out, I'm prepared to walk away and let you find a life without me. But I want to be sure that, if that's your choice, you fully understand how it happened. I was involved with my boss. I couldn't just walk away and abandon him. I needed time to break it off without hurting him and my career!'

Ken bridled: 'But hurting me didn't matter, did it? I was supposed to say – yes, that's fine, you go on seeing him, sleeping with him – and I'll just wait until you're ready to move on, until it's my turn!'

Sheila's eyes flashed. 'It wasn't like that! You're the one who's not being fair! He'd done so much for me, and I was fond of him – of course I was! You're not thinking about my feelings! About the mess I was in! All I needed was time…'

The ten inches between them reduced to five as their tempers flared. Ken's fists clenched. 'Fond! Was that it? But that's not the worst! You were just so bloody naïve to take him in! He conned you with that bloody stupid story about his wife: how she - so conveniently - found out about the two of you and sent him packing to your door with…a bloody…' He was running out of words and breath.

'He'd nowhere to go!' The gap between them was now two inches and closing. Sheila's eyes were large and very close to his. Her fine cheekbones were flushed with understandable anger. Her blonde hair, cut so that it fell straight but curved in at the ends, was caressing her shoulders as she leaned in towards him. 'You can't leave a friend on the streets when he's nowhere to go! I never meant him to stay and you know that! I told you he was out as soon as he found somewhere to live!'

She hadn't. He remembered none of that – only the fury he felt when she broke the news. He reached out to hold her, to impress on her the pain he had felt. His hand closed over her bare shoulder. The touch of his hand on her skin sent a shiver through her. Ken, in turn, experienced a sudden surge of energy as the softness of her flesh registered on his consciousness. Suddenly, without either intending it, the distance between them melted away. His lips found hers in what quickly became a pressing, burning kiss. Her hands snaked around his back and felt the firmness of his body. He cupped one of her breasts. Their eyes closed. Feelings, so long suppressed, were suddenly, passionately, released.

Five minutes later, a delivery boy drew up on his motor bike. He walked to the door, checked the address, and rang the bell. No answer. He knocked on the door then tried the bell again. He shrugged. This was where he'd been told to deliver the food. It was paid for. He'd done his job. No tip then. He dumped the paper carrier on the doorstep; took a photograph with his phone to make sure there'd be no come-back; kicked his bike back into life and sped away.

Early the next morning Sheila, as she was leaving, almost tripped over a carrier bag filled with a Chinese feast for two, cold and congealing. Ken had let her shower first and then, as he enjoyed the warm water pouring over his body, he tried to allay his doubts. Without anything being said, he felt that he had made a commitment to a relationship he was still unsure about. But why not? She was intelligent, beautiful, and amazing in bed. He knew that most men would envy him. He convinced himself that he owed it to her (and him) to give it a go. Maybe in time he'd be grateful that she'd stuck with him after all they'd been through.

The phone rang. He turned off the shower and wrapped a bath sheet around himself. It could be a breakthrough in the case. But it wasn't. It was Wendy, the crime reporter from the local rag. 'Hi Ken!'

'Wendy?'

'Yes – is this a good time?'

'You've just dragged me from the shower.'

'I'll try not to let my imagination dwell too long on that!'

Ken assumed she was joking. She'd never shown any interest him except as a source of information. They'd last met a couple of days earlier. They had parted on uneasy terms after she had spent much of the evening criticising his treatment of Sheila. At the time, he had resented this. But now, maybe she'd been right. Maybe.

'Are you OK?' He wondered why she was calling so early.

'Yeah. I thought I'd let you know we're planning to lead with the alien story. Any angles you can share with me?'

Ken wasn't sure he'd heard properly. 'Aliens?'

'Yep. Extra terrestrials invade Dorset! That's the line we're taking. I was told your team is handling it. So I thought I'd give you a ring.'

Ken shook his head. 'Sorry Wendy. Know nothing about it. Is it a joke?'

'No joke. A farmer in Tarrant Hinton saw them trying to steal her sheep and frightened them off with a shotgun. Then they struck again last night near Bere Regis.'

'Yes - but aliens? Can't be. Not really!'

'That's what we thought. But then it turned out the Bere farm had CCTV. We've got video!'

'Of aliens?'

'Yep. It's a great story.'

'But why would they steal sheep?'

'Maybe they think they're the master race here. That sheep are ruling us. Or they want to breed from them!'

'Or discovered a taste for shepherd's pie! Sorry Wendy, I can't help. I've been tied up with this murder on the ferry.'

'Ah well – what about that case? Any progress?'

'Early stages yet. It's mainly Hampshire's responsibility. I'm sort of hoping they solve it without much input from us. Look – I'll get to the office and see what's up. Get back to you then.' With Wendy off his back for a while, he finished dressing then rang Trevor, the oldest and relatively senior member of his office team. But Trevor had little to say about aliens. He still thought them a hoax. He was much more excited about a development in the case of the murder on the ferry. Something very odd had turned up.

Nikki removed the mask that covered her eyes, keeping them cool and moist at night, and stared blankly at her bedside clock. Half past ten in the morning. It had been close to midnight when she had snuggled down into her princess bed with its silky satin sheets and soft duvet; the canopy draped above the pillows a froth of lace. There was no sign of her husband. It was more than a year since she and Michael had shared a bedroom. His snoring had got too much for her. He hadn't objected. The arrangement suited them.

He hadn't got home before she'd hit the sheets, having first taken a tablet to ensure a good night's beauty sleep. And by now he should be gone – back to the office. But as she raised her pretty head from the soft silence of the pillows, she was disturbed to hear sounds coming from the adjoining room. She wrapped a silk gown round her slim form and ran a brush through her hair. It wouldn't do to appear crumpled, even if she was about to confront a burglar. A girl has to look her best. She went on tiptoe past the dressing area and the ensuite bathroom to the bedroom door. She paused. Yes, she was right. The sounds were coming from the bedroom Michael used. She could hear drawers being opened, rustling noises, the muffled sounds of someone trying to work soundlessly. Nikki should have crept back to her bedroom and called for help. But curiosity proved too strong a master. She edged to the frame of the door and one perfectly made-up eye peeped cautiously into the room. It was Michael.

'What are you doing? Why aren't you at work?' She spoke with all the authority of the mistress of the house – someone who was entitled to have her empire entirely to herself on weekdays. Her husband turned and confirmed that the fall of perfect blonde hair and the one visible eye betrayed the accusing presence of his wife.

'I'm packing.'

'Packing? Why? Is it work? You never said!' Justifiable annoyance at husbands who omit to inform their better halves of their plans.

He turned back to his packing: 'No. It's time to come straight. I'm leaving! Now! Today!'

Nikki clutched the silk gown tightly round her chest. 'Leaving? Whayoumean leaving? Where you bloody going?'

'If you must know: if you haven't already guessed! I'm going to Olivia. To Olivia, full stop. I'm leaving. I'm through with you, you nagging, useless bitch!'

'You've been shagging her! How long? How many times?' She was livid with rage.

'Yes. I've shagged her. And it was bloody good! And me and you - we're finished! It's over! Her husband's dead and she needs me and so I'm off! And don't pretend you're surprised! We've been over for years!'

Too furious to respond with words, choking with rage, Nikki's elegant fingers, with their exquisitely manicured nails, closed around a large bottle of Dolce and Gabbani aftershave. Her expertise as a pace bowler in her schoolgirl cricket team became useful for the first time in thirty eight years as she launched the missile at her husband's unsuspecting head. It caught him on the temple and drew blood. The next object she grabbed was a comb and it too was sent unerringly to its target, but it was too light to cause any further damage. He screamed at her in anger: 'You bloody idiot! Are you mad?' He hastily closed his case and made off with it, only half packed, as she ran over to the bedside table and picked up a cut glass decanter, half full of single malt whisky. It smashed against the inside of the door as he closed it behind him.

But Nikki wasn't finished – far from it. So that tart Olivia had stolen her husband, had she? The fact that Nikki had seriously considered killing him a couple of days ago was not the point. She was younger than Olivia (just) and prettier. What had that slag got that she hadn't? Well, her husband now! She threw open a bedroom window and then tore into his wardrobe. Item after item of expensive, designer clothing found itself flying through the air to land in the flower bed below. She'd take the dog out there later and make sure he peed on them.

Finally, fighting for breath, a plan began to form in her mind. He had left her. Gone to the woman she had thought was her best friend. Well, there were things she knew that she could use against them. Their enjoyment was going to be short lived.

A woman wronged makes a formidable enemy. She picked up the phone, dialled 999 and asked for the detectives dealing with the case of the murder on the ferry.

Ken joined Jenny in the incident room and called the team together. 'Trevor, can you just go over the development you shared with me on the phone?'

'Yes boss.' Trevor stood up and adjusted his cardigan. Rather bizarrely it boasted pictures of reindeers. It was November. Still, Ken thought, Christmas seemed to come earlier every year. Trevor brushed hair from his brow and wondered if he should go to the barbers – but he hated getting it cut. 'We've two uniforms helping us with the interviews. It's not enough but they're a bit stretched with this royal business. One of them called on a lad in Wimborne. His name was on the passenger list we got from Hampshire: Kenzie Joyce. Kid's names get dafter every year! The lad said he'd never been there. Not gone to France at all. He'd been at school. He's eighteen. In the sixth form. The uniform asked to see his passport and he couldn't find it. We checked with the school, and they had him registered as present every day this week. So we checked with customs and his passport was scanned as coming back into the country when the ferry docked. It's just a bit odd.'

'Right.' Ken chewed his lip. 'So – could be he's lying, and the school has messed up. Not impossible. Sixth form attendance isn't always checked thoroughly. They're trusted more: treated more as adults. In which case he's a possible suspect. Or – someone stole his passport and used it. And that person could be our killer. We need to visit him again in any case. Not bring him in yet – he's young so we'll try a gentle approach. Nigel – ring his home and set up a meeting there in an hour. Jenny – you come with me. Trevor, get any more information you can from passport control – when did the passport leave the country for France? And Nigel, I'd like as much info as we can get on the Leverson's business interests. It could be that they owed money to someone. Or had wrecked someone's livelihood. Anything that would give a possible motive. And who benefits from his death? Check everything. And then there's this thing with the creatures from outer space!'

Trevor nodded, a twinkle in his eyes. 'Yes boss. Sarah went to see the woman last night.'

Sarah stood. 'I took a statement from her. She insisted she saw them. Frightened them off with a shotgun. I checked the gun. It had been fired.'

Trevor waved her to sit down. 'We did what we had to do. Went through the motions. Filed the report. It's just nonsense. But then we had another.'

Sarah filled in the details. 'Yes. This time they're on

CCTV. It's weird. boss. What would aliens do with sheep?'

Ken dismissed this. 'Nothing Sarah. Check out all the fancy dress shops in Dorset. Ask them if they've sold job lots of alien masks in the last few months. If they have, ask for copies of receipts. See if you can trace bank accounts. That should lead us to the gang.'

'And what are they doing with the sheep?' Jenny asked. The question brought a few sniggers from the more prurient members of the team.

Ken supported her. 'Good question. They're not going to keep them in fields. The marks on the fleece make them too recognisable. They must be getting them butchered. Nigel – check on all slaughterhouses in the area. Find out if they've had any unusual requests from men who aren't known to them as farmers. Okay – everyone clear about what to do? Off we go then!' And Ken and Jenny strode out to the car park to check on the mystery of the youth who had been to France and yet had never left Dorset.

In her office high in the same building, with a window that gave her a similar view of the rolling green hills and meadows of the county she was pledged to protect as the one in the Chief's office (but was smaller), Alicia plotted. Before her was spread the Chief Constable's latest expenses claim. She photocopied it and then countersigned the original for approval, as she was required to do. A short walk along the corridor to Jane's office. Alicia did her best attempt at a sweet smile. She fancied Jane, although she was, in her opinion, too slim, too pretty and too close to her employer. Alicia suspected that there was more to their relationship than was purely professional. Whether that was true or not, Alicia's intuition told her that Jane was, as the popular saying went, sweet on him. She would use this to her advantage.

'Hello Jane. I'm returning the latest expenses sheet, approved of course!'

Jane accepted it with a grateful nod.

Alicia's face crumpled into an expression that she hoped showed care and concern. 'He seems to have such a busy schedule!'

Jane melted. 'I know! I try my best to support him. He bears such heavy responsibility!'

'Oh, I know, I know! You're a treasure. He'd be lost without you!' Then, like a cobra, she struck. 'I'm wondering if there are any of his duties that I could manage for him – to make his life easier...'

'Oh, I don't know...'

'Maybe I could look over his diary, for the last, say, three months, and highlight any visits or mundane duties that I could, in future, take off his hands? He's under so much pressure and I'd like to help! Only with his approval., of course. But I could perhaps make a shortlist of matters he could leave to me? He is such a wonderful leader. He deserves our help. Don't you think?'

Jane did think – a wonderful man indeed. And maybe Alicia could help to take some of the strain off him. Give him more opportunities for breaks away from the office. Maybe breaks he would spend with his loyal secretary...? She couldn't see any harm in it. 'His personal diary? Would you need it for long? Obviously, I need it near me so that I keep it updated...' (And hug it to her bosom when there was no-one around to see.)

'An hour at the most! I'll bring it straight back!' And Alicia strode back to her office in triumph; the A4 sized, leather bound book clasped to her tightly strapped chest; her eyes glinting at her own cleverness. Soon she was cross-checking the entries against his expense claims. She had all the evidence she needed. Gleefully she copied week after week of diary entries, noting every occasion when claims were made for journeys or for meals that couldn't have happened. Her next port of call, in full sail and with all guns loaded, would be the office of the force's solicitors. And then the Commissioner. The battle lines were drawn. And, in her mind at least, the war was already as good as won.

Ken and Jenny pulled up outside a neat semi-detached house on the outskirts of Wimborne. They stared for a moment at the bland frontage, the neatly painted windows, the faux oak front door, the flowery curtains. It did not look like the stereotypical image of a murderer's lair, but this didn't faze them. Killers don't dwell in darkened houses with guns and axes propped up against the windows. Life would be easier if they did. Ken was a few minutes early, so rather than go straight in, he called base. 'Trevor, any word on the passport?'

A gravelly voice came back. 'Yes boss. We've been in contact with customs our end and the ferry company. Nothing from the French authorities yet, but we may not need it. The passport was taken onto the ship for the morning sailing on the 13th. It was registered as leaving the ferry and then getting back on it almost immediately for the evening sailing back to Portsmouth. Whoever had it can't have spent more than ninety minutes off the ship.'

Ken looked at Jenny. This was strange. Then: 'It sounds as if this was a planned attack then. Whoever did it, if it was the person with this passport, they travelled on the ferry with the express intention of killing someone. They knew the victim and they must have known his movements. It's the best lead we have.'

Jenny nodded. 'But still no motive.'

Ken sighed. 'Planned murders are usually for money, lust or revenge. I think we can rule lust out. Domestic killings are done on the spur of the moment, so that rules out family arguments or abuse. Well, let's see if we can find the missing passport.' They left the car and walked up the short drive to the front door. Ken rang the bell. Shuffling sounds from within. A key turned. The door opened a crack. An attractive middle-aged woman peered out at them. She didn't seemed pleased.

'Mrs Joyce?' A bouffant of auburn hair nodded. 'Police.' Ken showed his warrant card. 'We'd like to talk to you and your son.'

The door opened wider. 'I don't see why. Already said. We know nothing about it. Will it take long? Kenzie's missing school!'

Ken tried to mollify her. 'We'll be as quick as we can. We just need to eliminate your son from our enquiries. We'll need a swab for DNA, a picture of your son, and just a few questions about the passport. Anything he can tell us.'

'Well, I suppose you'd better come in.'

The door opened just wide enough to enable Ken and Jenny to squeeze through. Nothing could have made plainer the unwillingness of the woman to allow them entry. Ken sighed. It was not the first time he had to cope with the fierce protection of a mother for her darling son. They followed her into the front room. A comfortable three-piece suite. Curtains, covered with tiny pink and red roses, held back by ties. Charming cushions carefully arranged. A spotlessly clean carpet, soft underfoot, in a shade somewhere between pink and beige that was hard to identify. A pale wood veneer adorned the G plan coffee table, on which a country homes magazine and a Jilly Cooper novel were intended to demonstrate that this was a place of refined good taste.

Slouched in one of the armchairs was the fruit of this good lady's loins. He stared sullenly at the two detectives. Ken tried. He held out his hand. 'Kenzie? I'm Detective Inspector Jones – please call me Ken – and this is my sergeant, Jenny Grace. We just want to ask a few questions. To clear you from our enquiries. And there may be information you can give that will help us find a dangerous criminal.'

Kenzie shrugged. It was clear he did not think he had anything to add and that this was a waste of his time. Jenny tried: 'Kenzie, we think that someone may have been using your passport. Is it missing?' He nodded imperceptibly. 'Do you know when it went missing?' A shake of the head. 'Where do you keep it?' Ken despaired. Was the child dumb?

Mrs Joyce decided that she had better intervene or she'd never be rid of them. 'It's always in his bedroom. In a drawer. There's no need to lock it up, is there? People don't keep passports in safes, do they?'

Ken wondered if they'd be better splitting the two of them. 'Jenny, could you go with Mrs Joyce and see where the passport was kept? Will that be all right Mrs Joyce?' Mrs Joyce's mouth opened then closed but no sound came out. Clearly it was not all right, but she was unable to think of a reason why. Jenny led her to the door. 'And maybe you can provide the sergeant with a photo of Kenzie while you're there? You must have plenty. He's a very handsome young man!' A dispassionate observer might have doubted the truth of this, but it struck the right chord with the adoring mother who seemed to warm slightly and made a noise that was not exactly a word, but the most positive sound she had emitted so far. Jenny turned and smiled, giving Ken a thumbs up as she made her way to the stairs.

Ken sat next to the youth and tried to establish contact. 'Do you like football? What team do you support?'

'Bournemouth.' Good. The child could actually speak.

'They're doing well this season!' A nod. 'Do you get

to watch them?'

'Just on telly.'

'That's a shame. Too far? Solanke's playing well this season. And they've got a lot of young talent.' Ken thought he saw a spark of interest; maybe he was getting through. 'There's a police office at the Vitality Stadium. For when the home games need security. I might be able to get you in to watch a game. Would you like that?' Vigorous nodding. Yes, there was a definite breakthrough! 'I'll look into it, I promise. But now, you help me. If someone got hold of your passport, who could it be? Who goes into your room?'

A dull shrug. 'Dunno. My mum.'

'Of course. But she wouldn't take it. Anybody else? Think hard. Whoever took it could have got you into trouble. They would have been trying to get you blamed for something they've done. Who else, in the past few weeks, has had access?'

'My friends come over. Nobody else.'

'Here's a pad. Can you write down the names of everyone you can remember going in there?'

Kenzie took the ballpoint pen and began to write, reluctantly. He obviously thought this a tiresome chore that had no point. Ken watched, grateful that he had got somewhere and stunned at the childish, scrawling writing that wandered over the paper like an errant spider searching for a doomed fly. He wondered if schools taught handwriting any longer. Jenny appeared, holding two photographs. Thankful to be finished, the two officers gave their thanks and left, Ken clutching this new, if barely legible, list of leads. As he left, he turned and repeated his promise to Kenzie that he'd get him into a Cherries' home game.

Nikki, frustrated now as well as furious, finally got through to the homicide team. Trevor was taking her call. He had little confidence that this would be useful. One of the more onerous tasks faced in any investigation is handling phone calls from cranks. Or people who want to help and think they may have something but are not sure what. Ninety percent of these are a waste of police time, but all must be acknowledged and logged. Patiently, he wrote down Nikki's name and address while chewing on his bacon sandwich.

'Now love, tell us what you think'll help us with our enquiries,' he drawled. 'Take your time. I'll write down what you say.' Expecting little, he turned his pencil, absent mindedly, in the sharpener.

'I can help you all right! I can tell you who did it! It was his wife! She told me she was going to rid 'erself of'im!'

Trevor sighed. Another nutcase. 'Get rid of him? Like – divorce him?'

'No. Kill'im! She said it'd be justifiable homicide! There were lots of us there! We all heard it!'

'When was this, love?' Trevor had broken the point on his pencil and reached for another.

'On Thursday! About three o'clock! It was our weekly get-together. We meet every week. For lunch, like. She said it then!'

Trevor put the pencil down. He wasn't going to waste any more time on this. Thursday was the night her husband had died. It was impossible that his wife could have been at a lunch date with these women and simultaneously have boarded a ferry in St Malo. He'd humour her for a while longer, then get rid of her. 'Have you known her long, love? How would you describe the relationship between her and her husband? Did they get on all right?'

'Did they bloody 'ell! She 'ated'im!' As she rose to her subject, her 'h's dropped out of sight. 'They were always arguing! She couldn't wait to be rid of'im!'

Trevor considered this. It was a new light on the relationship. He wondered what the quarrels were about. He offered the subject that most often caused disagreement between Trevor and his own better half. 'Argued a lot, did they? What about, love? Money, was it?'

'No!' Nikki laughed. Money was never a problem. At least not for Olivia. 'No – it was 'er son, Jason. He was always getting at 'im. Nothing he did was ever right. They 'ated each other!'

Trevor decided that this might be worth recording. He stopped chewing the end of his pencil and put it to the paper. 'Argued a lot then?' It was a new bit of information. Might be nothing, but it needed passing on to his boss. The more background intelligence they could gather, the better. It helped to build the picture. 'Tell me a bit more, love.'

Alicia was seething with rage. All her scheming had to be put on hold, all because of a stupid scare that was exciting the media. She had to prepare a statement and hold a press conference. Not because of the latest murder or because her boss had been fiddling his expenses to supplement his investments in the stock exchange – all that was still in a file on her desk, shared with no one. No, bloody aliens! The local rag had, that morning, run a full page spread on the reports of extra-terrestrial sightings. They'd even managed to get stills from the CCTV on some piddling farm that seemed to show Klingons – of all things – stealing sheep. Bloody rubbish. And why hadn't she been told about these pictures? Last she knew it was just a cranky woman trying to grab attention. And now TV crews and the national press were on their way. This was just the sort of crazy story they loved. Furious, she stormed into the adjacent office and bellowed at the occupants, who trembled in fear. 'Get me Jones on the phone! NOW!'

Ken and Jenny drove to Kenzie's school, unaware of the storm about to descend on them. Relaxed, Jenny looked out at the Dorset countryside as it unrolled before her. It was mid-November. The wildflowers that are such a feature of these country roads in spring and summer were no more, but this was more than made up for by the colours in the autumn trees. As the low sun caught in their branches, the leaves were a stunning combination of flaming reds, glowing yellows and simmering orange. As the car ploughed through the deep puddles of rainwater that had gathered in dips in the lanes, she dreamed they were in a small boat and Ken was whisking her away to a deserted island. But then she was rudely awoken by the car's phone.

'D.I. Jones?'

'Yes.'

'I have the Assistant Chief Constable for you.'

Ken grimaced and Jenny slowly shook her head. This could only be trouble. Their peaceful, leisurely drive was over.

'Ma'am?'

'Jones! What's happened about this aliens enquiry? Why am I not being kept informed? Do you imagine that you're running the force? That you can just do what you like?'

'Ma'am – as far as I know, nothing's happened. With respect, I don't know what you're talking about.'

Jenny curled up in her seat in fear. This was a dangerous line to take with the ACC – who was screaming down the phone. 'I'm talking about reporters from every national paper descending upon us! I'm talking about TV crews from every bloody television channel! There's even two from Japan! What I'm talking about is this story in the local press of another sighting, and actual pictures - film even - of what they claim are monsters from outer space! In Dorset! Why wasn't I kept informed? Why did I know nothing about it?'

Ken should have felt respect for the person who was berating him about this visitation from another planet, but in fact he was having difficulty keeping a straight face. The idea of Alicia, straightlaced and humourless Alicia, being interviewed on television about visitors from Mars struck him as hilarious. He tried to sound serious.

'Ma'am, we sent one of our team to the lady in Tarrant Hinton last night to take down details, but as for the CCTV pictures...' He glanced at Jenny. She was laughing and at the same time shaking her head and miming the zipping of lips. He took her advice. 'As for the pictures, they're news to me. We'll chase it up. I'll get in touch with the Dorset paper and find out where they came from. Then I'll get back to you immediately!'

There were a few seconds of silence as Alicia considered this. She didn't trust Ken but had no evidence that he was lying. Yet. 'Get straight back to me, Jones. I don't want to face the media scrum without knowing everything there is to know. Everything. And a full update on the investigation. Understand?'

'Ma'am. But we're on a significant lead in this murder investigation. It's urgent we...'

'Urgent! Don't tell me what's urgent, Jones! I tell you what's urgent! Get to it!'

'Yes ma'am. Right away!'

The connection was severed. Jenny was soothing. 'Should be all right. She won't know that we only found out this morning. But you'd better get on to it!'

Ken knew she was right. 'Can you check at the school on your own? I'll drop you there, then head back to the office to find out what I can. I'll get a patrol car to pick you up.'

'Sure.'

They drove through the main gates, following the signs that directed parents picking up their offspring. This left them some way from the main entrance, so Ken took a diversion and drew up outside the front doors. As with all schools nowadays, it wasn't possible to walk straight in. Jenny found herself in an entrance hall with locked doors ahead of her and a glass window to her right. Behind this was a friendly receptionist, who took her name and saw her ID before requesting that she wait for one of the deputies to attend to her. Only when he arrived, was she ushered through into the main school building. Here the head of year and one of Kenzie's teachers both confirmed that yes, he had been present on the two days in question. Images from the school's CCTV system backed up their claims. So Jenny left bemused. Who had been using Kenzie's passport? How had he acquired it? And why?

When Ken strode into his team's office, he saw his officers clustered around a computer monitor all watching the CCTV images from the farm. Trevor gestured to him to join them. The images were grainy. They'd been taken at night. But he could make out five, maybe six, individuals dragging sheep out of a gate. The thieves wore masks that gave them the ridged foreheads typical of Star Trek characters. But it wasn't only these masks that gave them the appearance of extra-terrestrials. There was a soundtrack of electronic noises that resembled the 'Doctor Who' theme tune, along with lights that flashed rhythmically. Ken wasn't surprised that, at first sight, people had been convinced that this was an alien visit.

Sarah touched his arm to attract his attention. She was new to the team and keen to make a good impression. Becoming a detective constable had been a big step for her, only two years out of college. She had close-cropped hair and round glasses with metal frames. She reminded Ken of Yoko Ono, though there was nothing Oriental about her. 'I contacted four shops that sell party clothes, sir,' she told him, her eyes wide. 'One in Bournemouth stocks alien masks and costumes. They said they had an order for six masks, Klingon ones, a week ago. The man remembered because the order was just for masks. Normally customers want the full getup. And it was odd to get a group order like this. They only usually come when there's a cricket match – like a test match, an England game...' Ken nodded. He understood. 'That's when a group of friends go to the match all dressed the same, as pantomime dames or Shrek. The shopkeeper thinks they like to go in a group – it gives them the confidence to make fools of themselves.'

Ken needed more information. 'Good Sarah. That sounds like the shop. Does the owner have records of the people who bought them?'

'Not names or an address. He doesn't need customers to give those unless they're hiring costumes. And this was a straight sale.'

'Damn.'

'But he has got a debit card slip. They paid by card!'

'Have you got it?'

'Yes, boss. It's here. I've only just got back! But it's no use. It only has the last four numbers of the account...'

Ken swung round. 'Trevor! Good work Sarah, by the way.' Sarah glowed. Her eyes, magnified by the lenses of her glasses, sparkled. 'Trevor – we need to trace the bank and then identify the account that was used – the last four numbers should be enough. Give them the name of the shop and the date and time! Listen up folks!'

The team swung round, giving him their full attention. 'Like it or not, we've been instructed by the ACC, bless her, to concentrate our time on these sheep rustlers. She's facing hassle from the press. So let's show her what we can do. And the quicker the better!' They all nodded. They all knew the ACC – and were wary of her. She'd been a thorn in their side before. 'Nigel – they must have used a large vehicle to get away with that many sheep. How many were taken?'

He called across from his desk, 'Ten, boss.'

Ken nodded. 'At a hundred pounds each as carcases, that's a good night's work. They'd need a van or trailer just large enough to take ten sheep. If they could have fitted more in, they'd have taken more. So Nigel, look at all the traffic cameras in that area on the night of the 7th and check for animal trailers. There can't be that many on the roads at two in the morning. See if you can get number plates.'

'On it, boss!'

'Jack – contact all the local abattoirs. They'd need somewhere to slaughter the sheep and then a butchery. See if any have been approached lately with requests to deal with small numbers – probably from someone claiming to be a farmer, but not someone they've dealt with before. The rest of you, help Nigel out with the traffic cameras – we need to get results fast!'

And with a chorus of yes boss, right boss, the team swung into action. Ken gave a sigh of relief and picked up his phone. It was time to bring Alicia up to date. He had to make it sound as if real progress was being made, although to date all he could know for sure was that aliens were not involved. At least she'd be able to assure the press and the good people of Dorset that they were not facing an invasion from outer space.

'Jones?'

'Ma'am.'

'You've got something for me?'

'Yes ma'am. We've found where the gang obtained the masks they used to disguise themselves. We've contacted the source and they haven't got names, but we have a card receipt. We're in the process of contacting the bank to track down the account holder's name and address. I'm confident we'll have at least one arrest before the end of today.'

'So I can reassure the press that a) no aliens are involved and b) arrests are imminent?'

'Yes ma'am, though it would help if you waited till we've obtained the address and followed it up before you release those details – in case it spooks the offenders and makes our job harder.'

'The media briefing is at three this afternoon, Jones. If you want the suspects locked up before then, you'd better get a move on.'

'Thank you, ma'am.' Ken looked at his wristwatch. That gave them just over three hours. It was hardly enough. And if he could have seen the woman at the other end of the line, he would have been surprised by the way the expression on her face changed from one of extreme annoyance to one of inspired cunning. The ACC had been wondering how to approach the matter of the Chief's overblown expense claims without any blame falling on her. She'd just realised that DI Ken Jones could provide her with a way of achieving her objective without anyone guessing her role in it. She was still on the phone.

'By the way, Jones – I know you're concerned to track down any possible evidence of corruption in the force. It's one of your areas of particular interest, am I right?'

'Yes, ma'am. I believe it our duty to uphold the law, not break it.'

'Exactly. Very laudable. Well; when you've tied up this aliens case, I want to speak to you about another matter...'

Ken was suspicious. Why him? The ACC was no friend of his. There were others she could call on. If she had picked him out, there must be a motive. And he doubted that it would go well for him.

'Certainly ma'am. I'll do my best.'

'I'm sure you will Jones. I'm sure you will!' And she almost purred with satisfaction as she sat back and contemplated her own brilliance.

Ken swung the car into a road of modest semi-detached houses in Hamworthy. He pulled up outside number 12. The blue lights, normally concealed in the car's radiator grill, cast an eerie glow on the front door. It had been painted white a long time ago and the blue gave it an almost disco like fluorescence. The curtains were all closed. Either the occupants liked an afternoon nap, Ken thought, or they had something to hide. Jenny checked the address the bank had given them. Yes, this was where the account was registered. Something about it didn't look right. The front gardens of other homes in the street, all equally small, were adorned with small ornamental bushes and sometimes potted plants. The spaces between sported a small square of lawn or paving. This frontage was characterised by its profusion of weeds, brambles, and discarded flowerpots. The paint on the windows was peeling and part of the guttering had given way so that a long damp stain adorned the front wall, dark and wet against the pebble dash.

As one, they opened the car doors and swung out. Just as they were about to walk through the gap where a gate had once stood, they were accosted by a ruddy faced man in a very loud jumper. Having spotted their blue lights, he'd thrown open his front door. His home was the adjoining semi to the one Ken and Jenny were approaching. 'At last! You've tekkken long enough!'

Ken turned to face him. 'I'm sorry sir – we're on police business.'

'Aye, I know you are. I called you! Two bloody days ago! Why's it tekken so long? We pay our rates, you know!'

Jenny decided she'd try to calm him. 'I think there's been a misunderstanding, sir. You say you called the police? What was the problem? Maybe we can help after we're done here.'

This was a man on a crusade. He had right on his side. Great offences had been committed. He was not to be put off by promises of maybe and after. 'Problem? Aye there's a bloody problem all right! You need to look round the back and see what we've got to bloody put up with!'

Cogs began to turn in Ken's brain. Maybe this man's complaints and the aliens could be connected. 'Round the back,' he offered. 'What's round the back?'

The man gave a look of total disgust. 'What's the point of phoning the effing police if they get here and don't know why they've come? What I told you about! When I phoned you! Two bloody days ago! The noise! All day and all night! We've hardly slept for it! And the stink! It makes you bloody puke!'

'There's a yard at the back? A back garden?' His team had had no success with the local abattoirs. The ones who remembered being asked to slaughter a dozen sheep all stated that they had refused. They didn't take livestock from an unregistered source. The small numbers involved weren't worth the risk of court action. Could it be that the thieves were still trying to unload their spoils? 'What's in there?'

'I dunno. They're covered up. Hundreds of'em. Stinking to high heaven. We don't mind pets. Got a dog misself. But this takes the bleeding biscuit!'

Ken took control. 'If you wouldn't mind going back indoors, sir, we'll take it from here. You can leave it to us to get to the bottom of what's going on.'

'Aye, all right. But I want to know. I want to know what's up!'

Jenny spoke quietly, as if confiding in him. 'Don't worry sir. We'll make a full inspection and report back to you *personally* before we leave!' Satisfied for the moment, but still grumbling under his breath, the man, back on his doorstep, looked up and down the street, as if checking for support, before retiring inside where he could boast to his long-suffering wife of the dressing-down he'd given to the effing useless police.

Jenny smiled and looked up at Ken. 'Nice. This is one of the great British public we're here to protect!'

Ken gave a rueful smile in return. 'And we protect them all – whether we like them or not!' Jenny started to move towards the door, but Ken stopped her. 'We don't know how many there might be inside – if anyone. If it's all four of them, we'll be outnumbered. Let's call for back-up and, meanwhile, maybe sneak round the back and find out what they're hiding there.'

They looked up and down the road. To gain entry to the lane that ran behind the houses, they would have to walk fifty yards to a side turning.

It meant passing the house with the annoyed – and annoying – neighbour. As they did so, Jenny noticed the net curtains twitch. She smiled and gave a little wave. No harm in being friendly. The curtain was swept abruptly back in place.

An alley ran between high fences; each gate signified the back entry to a garden. They counted the gates until they reached the one that belonged to the house in question. Unlike the other gardens, that showed evidence of bushes and fruit trees above the fence line, this seemed to be occupied by a tent like structure made of black, waterproof plastic. They could only glimpse the top of it. Ken gripped the top of the fence and lifted himself by his arms so that that he could glimpse over it. He saw that the tent covered most of the visible area. It was about ten feet by twenty. But it wasn't the structure that caught his attention. It was the strong stink of animal droppings, along with the loud bleating of many distressed animals. 'They're here all right,' he told Jenny. 'We'd better call the RSPCA while we search the house. Let's see if uniform are here yet.'

By the time they had made the way to the front of the house, two patrol cars were drawing up. Satisfied that they had enough numbers to cope with any possible resistance, Ken knocked on the front door. Jenny took two uniformed officers round the back in case any of the occupants tried to escape from the rear. The arrival of the cars had alerted more of the neighbours to the fact that something was going on. A small crowd began to gather.

'POLICE! Open up!' Ken hammered again on the door and waited for a response. At first there was none. Then he heard a scampering noise from somewhere inside. Ken decided this was clear evidence that someone was evading arrest, and it might be enough reason to justify a forced entry. There was also the welfare of the animals to consider. Yes, he was confident that this situation warranted the use of reasonable force. 'Police! We need to ask some questions. Open the door or we'll force it open!' He put his head close to the door. He could hear noises. It sounded as if more than one person was trying to escape. He couldn't make out any words, but they were clearly agitated. Ken lunged at the door with his shoulder. It creaked and almost gave. He took a step back and kicked at the side of the door with all the expertise that had scored the winning goal in the inter-station cup competition last spring. There was a tearing crack and the door swung open, with splinters of wood still attached to the lock.

Ken strode in, followed by four uniformed officers. They began a search, room by room. Two climbed the stairs, shouting instructions as they went. The others, with Ken in the lead, left the hall and checked the living room. Empty. The kitchen- also empty, with no sign of recent activity. The kettle was cold. No half-eaten food. Shouts came from upstairs. 'We've found one of the masks, sir! But no-one here! All clear here!' Ken turned to the final door. He assumed it opened to a dining room or study. It was closed. This was where they were hiding. He could hear movement from within. He turned to the officers with him. His face was grim. 'Hold your tasers ready!'

'Sir!'

'Right! We're going in!'

Ken raised his foot and crashed it into the door – which shattered with the impact. With the tasers each side of him, Ken shouted, 'Police! You're under arrest!'

The occupants of the room made no effort to escape. They stood in silence, staring wide eyed at the officers confronting them. Ken turned and walked back to the main door, where Jenny was waiting, having left two uniforms at the back. 'You all right, boss? Okay? How many were there?'

Ken looked blankly at her. 'I don't know. About eight I think.'

Jenny started in surprise. 'Eight! Did they say anything?'

'Yes,' Ken responded. 'Yes, they said something. It sounded like baa. The room was full of sheep!'

'Bloody hell!' said Jenny. 'And we found ten more in the back yard!'

◆ ◆ ◆

They were back at the office within the three hours specified by the ACC. Feeling suddenly weary, Ken phoned Alicia. 'Ma'am, we've located the house where the gang were holding out. We have the sheep safe, eighteen in all, and they're with the RSPCA. One of the masks we found, we've taken prints and it's on its way to you. You'll be able to show it to the press to prove they weren't real aliens.'

'Good work, Jones. And the suspects – how many are in custody?'

'They weren't there, ma'am. But we have names and we've put out a call for them and their van. They won't get far.'

'Let's hope not. But good, Jones. That'll be enough to keep the reporters happy. I'm sure you know that I hold you in high regard.' Ken knew nothing of the sort, but wisely stayed silent. 'Let me get this business over with and then we'll talk about the other matter I mentioned to you.'

'Thank you, ma'am. I'll do all I can to help.' And he disconnected the call.

Trevor sidled up to Ken. 'I've got something for you on the ferry business. Might be nothing. I'll deal with it if you're pushed for time.'

Ken was feeling the strain of the past couple of days, but he knew that, if Trevor thought it worth mentioning, it wouldn't be a complete waste of time. 'I'll probably leave it to you, but fill me in.'

'It's a woman called Nikki, boss. She rang in while you were out. She's convinced that the wife is behind the killing. Says she heard her threatening to do it.'

Ken looked to Jenny for support. 'Not sure how she could be involved. She wasn't on the ferry. We have witnesses saying that she never left the house.'

Trevor nodded. 'What I thought. But I asked her to come in anyway to make a statement. She's in the interview room.'

Inwardly, Ken groaned. This was almost certainly a false lead. A woman with a grudge against the wife, trying to stir up trouble. Still, they had no other leads. He wondered if Hampshire were having more luck. For once, he thought of Jenny. He knew she needed a break. 'Go home, Jen. Get a decent night's rest. Trevor, I'll see her with you. I don't suppose this'll take long.' Trevor picked up a notepad and they trooped, reluctantly, to Interview Room 1.

Ken regretted immediately his decision to let Jenny go early. Her calm assurance when dealing with irate females was badly missed. Nikki jumped immediately to her feet as they entered, sending her chair crashing backwards to the hard tiled floor. Her voice was as strident as her ruby lipstick as she yelled at her two male interrogators, her dark blue eyes flashing with fury. 'Arrest'er! I know she did it! Lying, cheating cxxx!' She was a simmering volcano of rage. Wronged, betrayed, ruined by a woman she thought her friend. No lioness attacking a rival for the dominant male could have bared her teeth more menacingly.

Ken bent down to retrieve her chair and gestured that she could sit. With a loud sniff that indicated she was in no mood for idle courtesies, she lowered her shapely derriere onto the seat and crossed her arms across a bulging bosom. As she did so, her breasts were pressed together, emphasising her cleavage, a deliberate assertion of her femininity. 'I'm a woman that men lust after and fawn over,' it seemed to say. 'And I've been badly wronged and what are you going to do about it?'

Ken wasn't planning to do very much. 'Mrs. Sawston, you want to make a statement?'

'Nikki.'

Trevor wrote something down. Nikki thought it was probably her name. It was lucky she couldn't see it. Ken persisted. 'Nicola Sawston...'

'Not Nicola. Nikki.'

Ken sighed and pressed on. 'Mrs. Sawston, you want to make an accusation against Mrs. Leverson? The lady whose husband has tragically died?'

Eyes flashed fire. 'No tragedy to that bitch! As soon as he was gone, she installed my Michael in her bed! She'd planned it all along!'

Ken tried to bring an element of sanity to the discussion. 'Mrs Sawston, you're making a very serious accusation. Michael is...your husband?'

'My 'usband! Bloody right! If she thinks she's stealing 'im, she's another think coming!'

Ken found this hard to believe. 'And he's moved in with her?'

'Bloody right! Packed a bag as soon as he 'eard and told me: That's it! It's over babe! Well, there's stuff I know that'll put that slut behind bars if you lot do your bloody job right!'

This was odd. Ken agreed it was surprising that a woman who had just lost her husband, in a brutal killing, would the next day install another man in her home. But whatever accusation Nikki made would have to be balanced against the obvious – she was furious and likely to make up anything that would put the other woman in a bad light. Where was Jenny when he needed her! 'We'd like you to make a written statement. You maintain that Olivia told you that she intended to kill her husband. Were there any other witnesses? Anyone who could corroborate your story?'

'Bloody right there are!' Nikki crossed her legs and settled back into her chair. It seemed the police were going to listen and take her seriously.

A written statement! That'd be something. She had prepared for this interview thoroughly. Gone through her wardrobe for a garment suitably serious. She hadn't many that fitted that description. She'd finally settled on a dark blue trouser suit. It was from a well-known high street outlet and so not up to her usual high standards, but it had sufficed. Matched with a cream collarless top in silk she thought she looked the part. Then there was her hair and make-up. A tight ponytail pulled the blonde hair severely from her high cheek bones and perfect forehead. She had held back a little on the eyes. Nevertheless, when she fluttered them at the nice detective man, it looked as if two tarantulas had been attached to her eyelids and were waving their legs suggestively in his direction.

Yes, there were others who would back up her story. All her friends had been with her at lunch that day. And she was confident they'd come forward when they heard about Olivia and Michael. This was a crime that would bring them together. No woman would be anything but shocked by what Olivia had done. Stealing someone's husband was a step too far amongst women who secretly suspected they were clinging to their own partners only by their fingertips.

Ken and Trevor looked at each other in amused bewilderment after Nikki had left. Could they take her seriously? 'Trev, can you check out the other women on the list tomorrow morning and see if they back up any of this story?'

'Sure boss.'

But Ken was certain they would. Nikki had been too confident in her assertions. And what she'd said about the stepson. Jason, wasn't it? He was, it seemed, the main cause of the relationship breaking down. Olivia's husband had taken an increasing dislike to him, according to Nikki. Constant arguments. He'd refused to let him out in the evening if he was behind with his homework. Refused his demands for money beyond his meagre allowance. It could be just a stepdad coping with a difficult adolescent. Still, they had no other clues at all. It was worth following up. But then, Olivia couldn't have been on the ferry and her son was at school. It seemed hopeless. But Ken was prepared to clutch any straws, no matter how small. 'Trevor, have you got that list of names we got from the kid – Kenzie, was it? Let's see if Olivia's son was one of the boys on it. If he's one of Kenzie's friends, he could have taken the passport...'

Trevor rummaged through the pile of papers on his desk. Just as he thought he'd have to check the wastepaper-bin, it turned up under the booklet of internal phone numbers. 'Found it, boss.' He scanned it quickly. There were only ten names. 'Nope. Nobody called Leverson. He couldn't have taken it.'

Ken paused. 'Is there a Jason?'

Trevor checked again. 'Yep. There's a Jason. Wrong surname though.'

'He wouldn't have the same name, would he? He'd still have Olivia's name from her first marriage.'

'It's possible...'

'First thing in the morning, check on what her name was and see if it matches. If it does, we'll check with the school to see if he was there those two days. And if he wasn't, let's go through the video from the ship again with facial recognition software to see he was on board. It's a shot in the dark, but it's all we've got.'

'Right, boss. First thing.'

Ken was happy to leave all this till morning. He'd had a text from Sheila. She suggested a meal out that evening and then back to her place. He needed a break. It would be good to relax, not worry about feeding himself, and – eventually – a good night's sleep. He needed one. It would be too far to go back to his home in Blandford and then drive all the way to Bournemouth. He opted for a shower at the police gym and found a clean polo shirt in his locker. On the road to Bournemouth, he called Wendy at the Dorset paper and gave her the news about the Klingons. A little more than she would have got from Alicia's press briefing, but not enough to compromise the investigation. Satisfied he'd done enough to help her, his mind drifted to

Jenny. Sheila's revelation that she was carrying a torch for him had come as a complete surprise. He felt guilty as hell about the way he had treated her, although he had never intended to hurt her. Deep down he was aware that letting her leave early had been in part thoughtful and kind – but lurking beneath was a dark impulse to ensure that she was away before he set off to Sheila's that night. Their relationship was strengthening again, and he felt instinctively that Jenny didn't approve. And could be jealous. And he didn't want to upset her anymore than he already had.

He parked near the Italian restaurant Sheila had suggested: close enough to her apartment to be within walking distance, so they could enjoy a bottle of Chianti or Prosecco without worry. He was there first, so he found a table and ordered a glass of wine. The evening was drawing in, but from his seat near a window he could look out at the gardens that stretch down to the sea. They looked magical in the dark blue of the night: trees and bushes lit with a myriad of floodlights drenching them in azures, purples and greens. The wine tasted of ripening fruits and soothed his throat. He felt more at peace than he had done at any time in the past year. The reconciliation with Sheila had settled him. He felt grounded in a relationship that could give him the love and companionship he needed.

He still had reservations. A suppressed worm of

doubt still wriggled in his subconscious. But when she arrived, looking amazing in a black dress that flared round her hips and was short enough to show off her long legs; when he saw how other men looked up from their plates and stared at her in open admiration; when he saw how her long blonde hair swayed as it caught the light and seemed to radiate, he felt nothing but pleasure and desire for her.

Ken stood and pulled back a chair. She smiled and sat, her shapely legs disappearing beneath the table. He filled her glass and she touched it to his. And as she whispered, 'To us!' he agreed and, for the moment, she seemed the most perfect woman in the world.

Three hours later as they lay naked in bed, glowing and content after their lovemaking, Ken ran his fingers over the silky smoothness of her skin. He moved slightly over the cool and silky sheets to snuggle closer to her. They were made, she had told him, of bamboo rather than cotton, another example of the exotic nature of her apartment. Her breath sounded to him like a purr as she sank into slumber. It was only after his hand had finally come to rest on the left cheek of her bottom that he too began to drift to sleep. As he did so, unpleasant thoughts began to disturb the otherwise idyllic moment. If he were to forge a permanent relationship with Sheila, how true would she be? After all, she had been keen to leave her previous lover in favour of him. He would often be away all day and sometimes at night in his work. If another attractive man crossed her path, would she be tempted? Jenny had hinted at her unsuitability. Was she correct – or was she biased against a woman as attractive Sheila? With small, nagging doubts worming away at his happiness, he eventually gave in to exhaustion and drifted into an uneasy sleep.

The next morning, he was a few minutes late into the office. Sheila had suggested that they shower together. The result was, as she anticipated, this intimacy resulted in such obvious physical arousal that they had made love on the bathroom floor. He could still feel the sensation of cold tiles against the skin on his back as he addressed his team for the morning briefing. 'Happy Tuesday, folks. Let's start with what we've been told about Olivia's son, Jason, and his relationship with his stepdad. Jenny, did you sense any tension when we interviewed Olivia?'

Jenny was startled. She had been assessing the change in Ken. He seemed different, more self-confident, more of a swagger. She tried to focus on the question. 'Err – no boss. She gave the impression it was all fine – just a happy family! And she said he was at college…'

Ken nodded. 'But if it's true that Nikki's husband moved in with her the day after her husband died, it puts a different light on things. Nigel, can you run a check on the widow and her son? Check for any previous and do a full financial check? While that's ongoing, I think Jenny and me should pay Olivia another visit! Sarah – any more on the alien rustlers?'

Sarah sat up straight, pleased to be important. 'The RSPCA have taken the sheep, boss. They're letting a vet look over them before returning them to the farms. I've put out a description of the van and uniform are looking out for it. Nobody's returned to the house yet, so they must be all be together, hiding out somewhere.'

'It'll just be a matter of time,' Ken assured her. 'Check on the house owner's bank card and see where he's used it in the last day or two. That'll help to pin them down.'

'Right boss!'

'Then ring Jason's school and see if he was there every day in the past week. Trevor, check social media posts to see if there is enough similarity between him and Kenzie for him to have used the same passport.'

Trevor waved a hand dismissively. 'Already done, boss. Waste of time. Got the image from the passport office. The picture is out of date. It just shows a young lad, looks about twelve. Any older boy could have used it and got away with it, provided they were the same colour!'

Ken shook his head sadly. 'So much for border

security!' He remembered similar instances of girls leaving the UK to join ISIS, successfully using older girls' passports to hide their true age. 'Okay, so Jason could have been on the ship with Kenzie's passport. Run facial recognition on the ferry videos.'

'Already running, boss. I'll let you know if owt comes up.'

'Good man. Okay Jenny – let's go. Don't let her know we're coming. Let's make it a surprise!'

Jenny felt awkward as Ken whisked her along the Blandford bypass and onto the narrow bridge that led to Durweston, a tiny village that is unique for its custom of shroving. Every Shrove Tuesday, children from the local school parade around the cottages singing and begging for titbits. The song goes back into the mists of time:

"We be come a shroving

For a piece of truckle-cheese

Or a piece of bacon

Of your own making

So light the fire and het the pan

For we be come a shroving"

But nothing so quaint as this was on Jenny's mind. She was very aware of the subtle change in her boss. And she feared he had taken a path unlikely to lead to a blissful destination. Jenny was fighting not only her own prejudice against Sheila, but also her own feelings for Ken. She had to convince herself that her doubts were well founded and not based on jealousy. Her fear of this kept her silent as they swung right into Sturminster and then on to the impressive church at Marnhull. She closed her eyes and tried a silent prayer, but words wouldn't come. At present, she convinced herself, she was content to be single and devote herself to her career. It was less than two months to Christmas. She had already planned to spend a few days in Croydon with her family. She knew how proud they were of her and of her recent promotion to sergeant. She'd make sure she did nothing to let them down. Melanie – a friend from training college – had tried to persuade her to go to Ibiza with a group of pals and have a riotous Christmas with them. But maybe she was getting old (although only just thirty). She couldn't rustle up any enthusiasm for it.

She was jolted out of her preoccupation with Ken and her love life – or lack of it – by the phone in the car beeping. It was Trevor, with news about the Klingons. 'A number recognition camera has picked up the van, boss. It's on the A31 heading towards Ringwood. Doing nearly eighty. Flat out I reckon. They must have twigged we're on to them. Making a run for it!'

'Good news, Trevor! Let's cut them off and bring them in!'

'We've got one car trailing them and another waiting near the Salisbury slip road. We'll pull them over when they get there. Should be any minute! Unless a UFO plucks them up into the wide blue yonder, they're ours!'

'Thanks Trev. Let them cool off in a cell for a while. Meanwhile, get forensics to go over the van. It should be full of stuff we can use against them. Sheep droppings if nothing else!' They'd reached the tight left turn to Fifehead Magdalen. Ken drove carefully down the narrow lane.

They pulled up at the heavy iron gates. Jenny said she'd do it. She was glad to get out of the car and use her legs. Pressing the intercom, she heard a soft buzz at the other end. No response. She tried again. Another few seconds and it crackled into life. It wasn't the domestic this time. It was Olivia. She sounded happy and excited. She wasn't expecting them. She was waiting for someone else. 'Michael darling! You're early!'

Jenny couldn't help smiling to herself. No, it wasn't the lover she had taken so soon after the death of her beloved husband. Far from it. She responded flatly, 'Not Michael. It's Detective Inspector Jones and Sergeant Grace. We have some further questions. To tidy up a few loose ends in our enquiries. Could you open the gates, please?' She heard Olivia utter a barely audible obscenity. The intercom went dead. The gates began to swing open. Ken and Jenny shared a brief meaningful glance, and then they drove up to the gloss black double doors that were firmly closed. Ken showed some impatience as he hammered on them and it wasn't long before the right door was opened. Not by the servant, but Olivia herself. She didn't seem pleased to see her unexpected visitors.

'You'd better come in. I haven't got long.'

'We'll be as quick as we can,' Ken promised her, tactfully. 'It's just that some new information has turned up and we need to check it with you.'

Slightly mollified, Olivia swung round and waved for them to follow her, through the hall, to the drawing room. She threw herself down onto a sofa, reclining like a twenties star of the silent screen, and made a gesture that implied that they were allowed to find a seat and get the interview over as quickly as possible. Jenny perched on the edge of an opulent Laura Ashley armchair, notebook at the ready. Ken remained standing, preferring to tower over his victim. 'You told us that your marriage was happy. But we have new information that you had frequent arguments with your husband and that your son, Jason, had a very troubled relationship with David.'

Olivia's pretty features contorted into angry fury. 'Who said so? Who's been spreading vicious, nasty lies?' Realisation dawned. 'It was her, wasn't it! That bitch! The effing cow! I'll tear her bleeding eyes out!'

Jenny tried to intervene. 'At this stage, we can't divulge our source. We're not accusing you of anything. This is a chance for you to refute these allegations...'

'Refute! I bloody do! That lying cow! She should mind her own bloody business!'

Ken stared hard at the distressed woman, her trophy wife sweetness slipping away like a magician's cloak to expose a bitter, foul-mouthed chimera. Once again, Jenny's thoughts turned to that last training session. The lecturer had insisted that they should reassess their ideas on psychpathic behaviour. It was present in as many women as men, it seemed. And at that moment, Olivia seemed to fit the description he'd given. 'They are more of a potential threat than we ever expected,' he had told his disbelieving audience. 'Coldness and lack of empathy are accompanied by thrill seeking in personal relationships. They use verbal aggression, manipulation, and seduction to get what they want.' Suddenly, Jenny saw Olivia not as the well-bred, refined, upper class lady she had seemed at first, but as a selfish and determined woman who could, perhaps, fit this description of a dangerous psychopath.

Ken. too. sensed something dark in her. Now was his chance to increase the pressure. The prey was roused. It was time to move in for the kill. But at that moment his phone rang. He glanced at the screen. It was Trevor. Ken didn't want to lose the advantage. He passed the phone to Jenny and indicated that she could take the call. She nodded and left the room with a mute apology to Olivia. Then Ken asked the question that would undo all Olivia's protestations of devotion to her dead husband. 'When you came to the intercom, you said *Michael*. You were expecting Michael. And you called him darling. *Is that you, darling?* So, tell me. Who is he?' Olivia's face paled. Her eyes flashed from one side of the room to the other, like a cornered rat. Her lips parted but no sound came.

In the hall, Jenny returned the call. 'Trevor. What you got for us?'

'Is that you Jen? It's about the boy – Jason. I used his social media pages to get a full face and then ran his image through the CCTV footage from the ship. We've got positive ID.'

Jenny gasped. 'He was on the ship?'

'Oh yes. We've got positives from the self-service cafeteria on board. And from the overnight seating. That's where the passengers spend the night if they haven't paid for a cabin. And then – you're going to love this!'

Jenny was in no mood for guessing games. 'What is it?'

'I'll send it to you. It's you leaving the ship.'

The video came up of Jenny and Ken in the crush of passengers exiting the ferry. Jenny pressed on the arrow to start the film. She watched people carrying luggage, pushing and shoving. Then the picture froze. She saw a close-up of the young man with a shock of blonde hair who almost knocked her over in his haste to leave. For a moment she was stunned. Then: 'That's him? Oh my God...!' She remembered him. He had seemed so desperate to get off the ship – to escape?

'Yep.' Trevor was amused. 'Olivia's son. The one his mum said was at school. Who'd have guessed it?'

Her first impulse was to face Olivia with the news. She walked down the hallway to an array of family photographs in joined-together frames.

There he was – in two of the pictures. The boy with the shock of hair, huddled up with his mother on a beach. Sitting uncomfortably with both parents on a sofa at a party. She lifted it from the wall and walked back into the drawing room. Ken was grilling the unhappy mother. 'Several witnesses have stated that you threatened to kill your husband the day before the murder. Are you denying that happened? That you made the threat?'

Olivia was furious. As she tried to make sense of this, she also had to come to terms with the fact that women she thought of as friends had turned against her. Had even, it seemed, gone to the police and reported on her. As she struggled to counter the detective's concerns about her, she was also discovering truths about the fragility of relationships, founded on little more solid than a mutual interest in the purchase of trivial things – from clothes to make-up. And in these few shocking seconds, she realised more: that trophy wives are deeply insecure. Each one secretly afraid that the superficial grip they each have on a husband could be lost as easily as it was won. And when one stole the bread winner from another – that was a step too far. A little flirting was nothing but harmless fun. Even a brief affair was something they could all take part in and enjoy.

But a permanent separation – to take him into your home and deprive one of the sisters permanently of her income – that was a step too far. The death of David had changed their relationship irrevocably. Oliivia had moved, without being conscious of any change, from being a close ally and confidante to being a serious threat. She was now an attractive and wealthy widow. No marriage was safe anymore.

Ken pressed on, wanting a response to his question. 'A number of witnesses, Olivia. We are investigating a murder. We must follow up every line of enquiry, no matter how upsetting.'

Olivia found strength in the bitter anger that surged up inside her at the thought of friends so disloyal. 'I may have said it! A joke, that's all! Those bloody bitches! I can't believe they said that! They knew I was joking!'

Jenny stepped in. 'Your son – Jason, isn't it?' Olivia stared at Jenny, and the photograph she was pointing towards her, so angry that she was unable to focus on the question. 'You said he's been at school for the past week.' Olivia, blank, opened her mouth but no sound came out. 'These photographs are of Jason, am I right?' She thrust the picture frames toward the distraught woman, a finger pointing at the boy. Olivia said nothing, just stared at her in confusion.

Jenny turned to Ken. 'We've just received these stills from the CCTV cameras on the ferry.' It was Ken's turn to be surprised. There the boy was, in the queue to leave the ship, pushing past them. Jenny stepped closer to Olivia so that she too could see the image. 'So how do you explain these pictures that show your son on the ferry? How could he be at school and on a return trip to France simultaneously? And how could you not be aware of it? It was your debit card that was used to purchase the tickets!'

Olivia gained a moment of strength from the fact that this was her house – her drawing room. Her castle. Time to fight back as far as she could. 'I know nothing about it! It might not be him! Someone looking like him! He wasn't...he can't have been...'

Ken took her arm. 'I must ask you to come with us to the station. We need to continue this under caution. You may want to contact your solicitor.' And Olivia did. Sweating profusely, she struggled with her phone. Her fingers suddenly weren't working well. It took her several attempts to get through. And the message she sent caused similar panic at the firm of Delware and Conroy, when she was put through to her trusted Mr Forbingham. Unfortunately for her, this ancient firm was adept at handling the financial affairs of its clients, but had little expertise in criminal law. Ken continued, 'We'd like your permission to search Jason's room.'

Olivia shook her head. 'No! You've no right!'

'I'll take her to the car, Jenny.' Ken judged that the suspect was too distracted to attempt to escape and did not cuff her. 'While I do that, get on to the office and get a warrant.' His sergeant nodded and rang Trevor. Under the circumstances it would be just a formality to obtain a search warrant. And so, as Olivia was led away in tears, Jenny took the initiative and walked up the wide stairs to the first floor. She found everything about the house soulless. No money had been spared, but it was like walking through the pages of a posh homes magazine. The paintings were bland, and chosen, not on merit, but because they matched the wallpaper. The ornaments were expensive in a glitzy way, but meaningless.

There was nothing that had been purchased with the heart. No objects of sentimental value, kept because they reminded the owner of a beloved grandparent or lost friend. It was more a show home on an exclusive housing development than a home. She tried one door that opened onto a fully tiled shiny, shower room. The next was a guest bedroom. It looked as if it had never been used. Cushions were piled artistically on a bed that was covered with a gold duvet. The carpet, deep and white, looked as if it had never felt the tread of human feet. Then she found a room that was clearly the domain of a teenage boy.

The walls were covered with posters. A large one of Taylor Swift faced the bed. She was wearing something very white, very spangly and very, very short. A large poster for Arsenal football club celebrated many of the star players. There were other posters Jenny couldn't approve of, but at least this was a room, unlike the rest of the house, that reflected a real person and his likes. She moved toward his laptop computer and began to put on blue plastic gloves before touching it … when she became conscious of someone behind her.

It was the maid. Jenny had forgotten all about her. She hadn't answered the intercom or come to the main door to let them in. She wore a plain black dress that reached her knees. Her hair was pulled back from her face into a tight ponytail. It was dark and her skin was light brown. Her eyes were black and her nose sharply pointed. Her looks belied her role. She had the air of someone shrewish and intelligent. Little would pass her by, although she would keep her opinions to herself. She stood in the doorway, clearly wondering what Jenny was doing in the boy's room.

'Madam?' Her large eyes stared at Jenny, distrustfully. Jenny was on uncertain ground. She hadn't been given permission to search by the homeowner and the warrant hadn't yet arrived, although she was sure it would. She decided to bluff it out, judging that the maid, who had come from somewhere abroad, would be unaware of her rights. 'What you doing? Why you here?' Jenny realised too late that she may have underestimated the young woman's pluck and loyalty. She pointed her warrant card at the maid.

'It's nothing to worry about. Your mistress is helping us with our enquiries. Into the death of the master.' Jenny felt, without any justification, that this archaic language was best suited to the occasion She had no experience of servants. 'I'm waiting for Jason. He must be terribly upset by what happened to his stepfather! They were very close, weren't they?'

The maid rolled her eyes expressively. 'They fight. All time. Nothing but yack, yack argue. He shits him in room.'

Jenny, puzzled, suggested, 'Shuts?'

'Ja – it's what I said. Shits him in room. Door close. Bang. Upset? No! They like cat and dog. Fight, fight, fight. The boy hate 'im! He back from school soon. I let him in?'

Jenny called Ken. 'Boss, the boy's back any minute. We need to take him in as well as his mother.'

'Roger that, Jen. I've still got Olivia in the back of the car. She's nearly used up all my tissues. Uniform are on their way to take her in. The search warrant's just come through. As soon as I can pass her over to them, I'll come in and join you.'

'Okay, boss. The maid's with me. She's blown the lid on this pretence of happy families.'

'Good work. Jen. We'll need a statement from her. Uniform's just arrived. See you in a sec.'

Jenny turned back to the maid, who was standing by the door, looking bemused. Jenny decided to assert her authority in case she objected to a search of the room. She pointed the phone rather aimlessly at the girl. 'It's come through.' The maid stared at her blankly. 'The warrant. It means I'm allowed to do a search of the room. Jason's room. It's all right.' Then very slowly, 'Do… you…understand?' The maid shrugged. It slowly dawned on Jenny that she understood perfectly and she wasn't bothered. She didn't care what the lady officer did … as long as she didn't have to clean it up afterwards.

Jenny began with the chest of drawers. She pulled the first one out and was surprised as the maid rushed up and helped her. It held mainly pants and socks. In the drawer below, hidden underneath football kit and a variety of sweaters, she found two girlie magazines. The maid grabbed these and held them by the corner, her face a picture of disgust.

'You want these? Evidence, yes?'

Jenny smiled and shook her head. Then turning to the bedside cabinet, she found what she sought. First the missing passport. Then, at the very back of a small drawer, a knife with a six-inch blade. The maid seemed less disturbed by these discoveries then she had been by the soft porn. But before she could comment, the doorbell rang. The maid scurried down to the hall and checked the intercom. It was Jason, with Ken close behind. She pressed the control that allowed the gate to swing open and waited by the door for them to reach her.

When they did, two things became immediately clear. Jason had little time for the maid, treating her with total disregard. And the maid had a very low opinion of Jason, curling her lip at him as he stormed past her. At the bottom of the stairs, he announced his arrival in a strident, 'Mam! I'm back!'

The maid, to her credit, attempted to bring him up to date with recent events. 'She not here. She gone to police...' But before she could complete the sentence the boy had gone. He took the stairs two at a time and crashed into his bedroom, only to find an imposing, dark-skinned lady standing next to his bed, holding a passport - and a knife wrapped in a sock. She smiled at him, reassuringly, as if she was accustomed to being discovered in teenager's bedrooms with the instruments of crime firmly in her grip. She slipped them into an evidence bag.

'Jason? My name is Detective Sergeant Jenny Grace. Call me Jenny.' The boy stared at her in astonishment, unable to find voice enough to call her anything. His skin visibly paled as the reality of discovering a detective - and incriminating evidence - in his room caused panic to swell up inside him. 'Sit down for a minute, Jason. I think we need a chat, don't we?' Jason was sure he didn't and was mentally cursing his luck. He had planned while at school to go out that evening and bury the two objects in a secluded part of their large garden. Under the compost heap, actually, where even the most determined seeker after truth would be unable to sniff them out. If only he'd had a couple more hours...

Ken appeared at the doorway and took in the situation immediately. He waited for Jason, who was unaware of his presence, to respond to Jenny's request. The boy sank down onto the bed, like an inflatable toy suddenly punctured. Jenny passed the evidence to Ken and sat beside the boy. 'I know it's been difficult for you. Your mum getting married again. And you getting a new dad. Lots of people have put in good words for you.' He looked up in surprise. She smiled to reassure him and continued with the white lie. 'They've told us how mean he was to you. He was, wasn't he?' The boy nodded mutely. 'He picked on you a lot, didn't he? And it's his fault you had to come and live here!' Another nod. He was beginning to trust her.

A pair of pensioners looking for somewhere quiet to live would be overjoyed to find themselves marooned in this idyllic Dorset hamlet, miles from civilisation, home to only eighty or so residents. All of them of mature years. But to a sociable teenager, into heavy rock and Arsenal, it was perjury. 'And I bet there were money problems.' Jason's eyes opened wide, and now he nodded vigorously. Here was a woman who understood him. To her, he could open his heart.

'Every bloody penny! I had to beg for it!' he almost sobbed. The injustice of it all! He knew his stepdad was filthy rich, but all his friends at school had more than he did. 'And I got jobs to do! He made me earn it! And he was loaded! He made me beg for lifts if I needed to go out at night! It was bloody unfair!'

Jenny nodded sympathetically. No agony aunt could have been more understanding. She might have felt sorry for him, as she led him further and further down the slippery road to confession, but it was hard. He seemed to her a confused kid with a grudge, yes, but also a spoilt brat who expected everything on a plate. And when the plate had turned out to be empty, he had done something terrible. 'But you had your mum, didn't you? She was on your side? Did she buy your ticket?'

Jason nodded, too caught up in his own self pity to realise that he was implicating his own mother in the crime. 'She stood up for me. They had blazing rows. I heard 'em. I did it for 'er an all. With 'im out of way, we'd both be better off. She'll get the money. She'll see me right!'

Ken watched this unfold in silence. He couldn't help but be impressed by the way that Jenny was adopting the role of a sympathetic ally, drawing the confession from the unsuspecting suspect whilst seeming to be a friend he could trust. She even read his rights to the boy without it seeming in the least threatening.

He had received news from Hampshire while in the car with Olivia. The post-mortem results were in. The victim had had a huge amount of alcohol in his system. Evidence from the bar on the ship backed this up. He had used his debit card more than twenty times in one evening to buy multiple shots. He had let someone in the cabin but was too drunk to defend himself. He had fallen on his front across the bed and been stabbed once in the back with a blade five or six inches long – one that matched the knife Jenny was still holding. The blow had been delivered with the left hand.

The wound was not enough to kill him. It wasn't deep, but it had severed an artery. He had lain sometime in a drunken stupor and slowly bled to death. There were some fingerprints, but none matched those on the police data base. Not surprising, if they happened to be those of a teenager who had never committed a crime before. He stared at Jason's hands. Now they were shaking, trembling with fear. They looked innocent enough, but, not long ago, had been firm enough to hold a knife and use it to take the life of his stepfather.

Jason was crying now. Jenny put an arm around him. 'You're young, Jason. Seventeen?' He nodded, choking with sobs. 'You just need to explain what it was like. How he treated you. You were driven to it, weren't you? We need you to come to the station with us and write down all that you've told me. It'll be your statement.'

The boy looked up at her, his pale blue eyes awash with tears. 'My mam?'

Jenny nodded. 'She's already there. You'll be able to see her.'

This seemed to reassure him. He stood and reached for his coat. He used his left hand. Ken smiled. The boy was left-handed. All the pieces were falling into place. As Jenny walked past him, he gave her arm a gentle squeeze. 'Great job! You were brilliant!'

She smiled back at him. 'Wasn't too hard! He's hardly a master criminal, is he?'

As they drove away, Nikki's husband passed them at the gates and drew up in his Audi. He hammered on the door, expecting Olivia to run out and embrace him. But the door remained firmly closed. Finally, he looked up and saw the maid, staring down at him. He waved to her and pointed to the door. She gave a wicked smile and raised a finger up at him. Then she vanished, leaving him out in the cold.

◆ ◆ ◆

Two Hampshire CID officers were waiting at HQ when Ken and Jenny arrived with their young prisoner. Ken had expected this. It was Hampshire's case, and they would now take it on. It was taking them all their time to convince Olivia that she couldn't call on the most expensive barrister in the land to support her. She would have to settle for a duty solicitor. She was under the impression she was a very wealthy woman. But it was highly likely that she was now penniless. She wouldn't get any of her husband's substantial fortune. If, as seemed likely, she was found guilty of perverting the course of justice by providing a false alibi for Jason and conspiring with him to murder her husband, she would get nothing. She wouldn't be allowed to benefit from the proceeds of her crimes.

Jenny felt nothing for her - an empty, vain, and selfish woman devoid of spirituality, living for nothing but material wealth. But she did feel slightly sorry for Jason as he was led away by detectives he didn't know. He looked tearfully at her as he was taken out to the car. They had formed some sort of bond in a short time but go he must, and Jenny gave him one last hug. But she hardly meant it. What he had done was unforgivable, no matter what the provocation.

But it was not only the CID officers who were waiting for them when they arrived back at the team office. No lesser person than the Assistant Chief Constable was standing patiently by Ken's desk, immaculate in her uniform. This was extraordinary. She was rarely seen out of her office and always summoned people to her, via her secretary and the telephone. No-one had ever heard of her making a social call before. But this, it turned out, was not a social call at all.

'Congratulations, Jones!' she almost smiled, though her eyes showed no sign of pleasure. 'Another excellent job. Hampshire are delighted. Another big plus for Dorset, solving their case for them!'

Ken chose, wisely, to spread the credit widely across his team, who were watching this exchange with considerable interest – and amazement. 'It was a joint effort, ma'am. The whole team played a part. We couldn't have done it without conscientious work on facial recognition, checking hours of footage, checking alibis: and Jenny did an amazing job with the boy, drawing the confession out of him.'

'Of course.' She waved her arm vaguely around the room. 'A credit to all you. But walk with me, Jones. There's something important that I need to discuss with you.' And with that she turned on her heels and followed the path back to her lair. Ken gazed round the surprised faces of his team and shrugged, before following her, reluctantly. As soon as he was gone, excited chatter broke out. What could she want? Speculation ranged from Ken being put on a superintendent course to a high achievement bonus payment for all on the team. It is from such baseless speculation that disappointment is born.

Alicia waited until Ken caught up with her. 'I have to accept, Jones, that you are proving a highly competent officer. I have had my doubts about you, I admit it. But despite my serious reservations, you are getting things done. You could prove a valuable asset to the force and further promotion is – well – not out of the question. But you are sometimes a loose cannon. I think it may be best if we worked more closely together. If you'll accept my guidance, restrain the impulse to do your own thing, I could forge a fine detective out of you. The sky's the limit, Jones, if you accept me as your guide and mentor!'

Ken didn't know how to respond to this. In theory it was good news. He had ambition, but he had principles too. And there were lines he couldn't cross and still live with himself. He respected Alicia because of her experience and superior rank. But did he trust her? No. She was wedded to the force and wouldn't accept any action that reflected badly on it. Whereas Ken, well, where he saw injustice, racial bias, or misogyny he couldn't help himself. His instinct was always to stamp on it. He walked alongside her, but if she was hoping for a positive response, she got nothing.

Alicia realised that Ken might be so overcome at her offer he was unable to voice his gratitude. She took his silence as assent and continued. 'Actually Jones, we can begin our partnership right away. You don't have to say anything. I know what this means to you. Come in. Close the door.' They had arrived at her office. Ken followed her in, feeling increasingly uncomfortable. The ACC was way above his paygrade. This sudden familiarity felt wrong in so many ways. She motioned him to take a seat. It was not the first time he'd been in her office. It was, though, the first time he'd been invited to sit. Always before he'd stood while being lashed by her tongue. He was perched on the edge of the leather chair, as if ready to flee at the first sign of danger.

Alicia opened a cabinet and produced two glasses, hand cut lead crystal judging by the way they caught the light. Almost as bright, Ken thought, as the highly polished chrome decoration on her uniform. She didn't ask him if he wanted a drink. She poured the amber liquid and passed him a glass. 'There's a particular case I want you to follow up for me. Just you, it's too sensitive to spread it around.' She stared at him, waiting for him to express an interest. He remained silent. She stared at a framed certificate on her wall telling her how clever she was and pursed her lips before continuing. 'It's a case of possible corruption in our own force. I know that's something that will concern you, Jones. Something you'll be keen to stamp on.' Again, she looked at him, her eyes narrowing. She reminded Ken of a cobra, poised and swaying slightly, attempting to hypnotise her victim before the fatal strike. 'It involves, I am sorry to say, a senior member of the force. Very senior. Very senior indeed.'

Ken suspected a trap. 'Ma'am you need someone more experienced for this. I'm still a rookie.'

Alicia mistook his reluctance for commendable modesty. She waved a hand dismissively and walked to her desk. She opened a manila file, at the same time giving Ken a look that signified that here was an item of vital importance. Ken put the glass down, untouched. He wasn't a great whisky drinker, even off duty. Dutifully, he drew the first sheet closer and scanned it. Then the second. It was immediately obvious that these were expenses claims, along with a page from a diary. It was even more obvious that these documents meant trouble. The diary entries were not those of a common traffic cop. The events listed were of high importance: meetings with county counsellors, a national conference, sessions with the police commissioner. Ken wanted nothing to do with it. Alicia purred:

'You see what's happening! Around half of these claims are genuine. The others cannot possibly be. The entries don't match. Between you and me, I know what's behind this. He's been fiddling these expenses for years and using the extra to invest in the stock market. We've enough evidence here to bring a case of gross misconduct!'

Ken closed the file. 'But why me? You seem to have all you need. You could go straight to the Crown Prosecutor!'

Alicia lifted one finger and tapped the side of her nose. She squinted at him in a way that she believed implied that she was being very clever indeed. 'No Jones. You don't understand. I can't be seen to be behind this. It may look as if I have a personal interest...maybe see it as a route to promotion. Nonsense, of course! Nothing could be further from my mind. But the outcome could mean me stepping in as acting Chief Constable until a permanent appointment can be made. And would that be me?' She continued, clearly meaning the exact opposite of what she said: 'I hardly think so!'

Ken understood all too clearly. It was obvious who had made these expense claims. And he was certain he wanted nothing to do with it. He had made himself very unpopular with many of his colleagues by exposing misogyny and wrongdoing by junior officers. But these had been serious offences. Women had suffered as a result of their actions – sometimes even been raped. The backlash had been unpleasant but a price worth paying. But to go through all that again because of a few errors in an expenses claim? He hadn't joined the police force for that. No. He was certain that the ACC was using him to further her own agenda. She planned to get all the benefit while leaving him to take the blame.

Alicia stared hard at the man she hoped would do her dirty work for her. It gradually dawned on her that he was not approaching the task with the enthusiasm she had expected. She decided it was time to raise the stakes. It was impossible for her to comprehend that Ken was just a decent human being. She assumed that everyone, deep down, was motivated by the same ambition that fired her. 'Of course, Jones, if you are my man...once I achieve the promotion – even if it turns out to be only temporary – you would be in a very strong position. A very strong position indeed. You'd have a friend in high places. I don't need to say any more, I'm sure!'

No, thought Ken, that's all pretty clear. He needed to play for time. If he was going to turn her down, he needed a good reason and space. 'I'm grateful for your confidence in me, ma'am. But this is a big thing for me to take on. Could I beg a little time to think it over? Especially as I've got this television interview to do tomorrow. It's sort of on my mind...'

Alicia beamed. Of course, that was the problem. He'd jump at the chance to be her stooge normally. The only thing stopping him from throwing himself at her feet in gratitude was this damned television thing. She understood, she thought, perfectly. She touched his arm reassuringly. Ken cringed. 'I completely understand, Jones. Believe me, you've no need to worry. You'll get all the support you need. HR will be there with you and the force solicitor. Just let them guide you. Don't answer any question without checking it out with them. But it's hanging over you: of course it is. Leave this for now and we'll talk again when the television business is done with!' Ken thanked her and slipped away. Safe for the present, but the day of reckoning had only been delayed. He needed advice from someone he could trust.

As he walked slowly back to his office, Michael, Nikki's husband, was driving home. He'd been refused entry to the house of his lover, Olivia. He didn't know why. But he needed to hedge his bets. If one door was closed to him, it would be best, he thought, to return home until he knew what his options were. As he drove through the gate, he considered his position. Should he go in all guns blazing, accusing his wife of unreasonable behaviour, insisting that all their problems were her fault? Or should he return as the penitent sinner, beg for forgiveness and promise a new start to their relationship?

What he saw in the garden made his mind up for him. All his clothes were scattered over the flower beds, soaking wet - probably ruined. Seething with anger, he stormed up to the door determined to bring her to heel – with force if necessary. Who does she think she is? He clenched his fists. He'd use a leather belt. He'd teach her a lesson she wouldn't forget in a hurry! He pulled out his keys and tried to shove one into the lock. It didn't fit. He tried again. He checked the key. It was the right one. Only then did he notice that the lock was new and shinier than he remembered. In the house, Nikki snuggled further down into her armchair and turned up the volume on the television, so that she couldn't hear the curses coming from outside. She had the house. She was confident of a generous divorce settlement. Did she need him? Oh no. The good life stretched before her, and she felt free as a bird… She had completely forgotten the pre-nuptial agreement he had made her sign before the wedding. At the time, it had seemed so unimportant. But it meant that much would be lost to her in the case of a separation or divorce - including the house. Revenge may be sweet, but can quickly turn sour!

Ken was back at his team room within five minutes of leaving the ACC. Seven pairs of eyes gazed at him expectantly. But Ken knew that the information he had was sensitive. This wasn't the audience he needed. 'Nothing to report, guys! She was trying to get on the right side of me! But the work you've all done on the ferry killing - she was over the moon! Well done everyone! Let's call it a day. Back in at nine tomorrow, okay?'

There was a chorus of thanks. They gathered their belongings and drifted away – a good half hour early. Jenny was the last to make her way to the door and Ken signalled for her to stay. She knew the ACC wouldn't have come to the office to take Ken away just to congratulate the team. She looked at him expectantly.

Ken took a deep breath. Before he could start, she sat on one of the swivel chairs and motioned to him to sit beside her. Jenny felt, instinctively, he had something very serious on his mind and this could take some time. Ken outlined the situation as briefly and clearly as he could, although some of the words were slightly muddled. He was still taking it in himself. It was a few seconds before Jenny responded. When she did it was damning. 'The bloody bitch! You see her plan, don't you? You do the dirty work, you get all the kickbacks, and she's sitting pretty! At worse, Ken, it's petty fraud! Why the hell should we get involved? Fraud! It's not a bit of you, Ken! If you drag the Chief through the shit, you'll be a marked man – and not just in this force, throughout the country!'

Ken nodded sadly. 'I wanted to share this with you, Jenny. I value your opinion. It's a bloody mess. Now she's shown me the evidence, I'm sort of duty bound to do something. But the Chief has been a public servant all his life. A dozen commendations. Whatever you think about him, he doesn't deserve to be forced out in disgrace with only a year or two left to serve. If it was something serious, an assault on a woman, serious allegations of racism, I'd be happy to act. But this…'

Jenny nodded, her face bleakly serious. 'You've got to get out of it, Ken.'

Ken sighed. 'But how? What do I tell her? I've gained a bit of time, but only a day or two.'

Jenny frowned. Then: 'Tell her you've got to wash your hair. It works for me when I want to get out of something!'

This was so ridiculous it cheered them both. They laughed together, but neither underestimated the difficulty facing Ken. 'Sorry, Jenny. It's not your problem. I'll think on. I'll work something out.'

'Hope so, Ken.'

Five hours later, after a good meal and a bottle of Rioja, Ken was lying in bed next to Sheila. She rubbed her naked body against his and ran a hand, temptingly, through his chest hair and down to his firm stomach. When he didn't respond as she expected she drew back slightly. 'Something on your mind?'

'What? No...not really.'

'Come on Ken. I can tell something's worrying you. It's not me, I hope!'

Ken raised himself a little on the pillow and stared at her. 'No. It's work. Something the Assistant Chief wants me to do.'

'Alicia? I thought she hated you!'

'Deep down I think she does. But she wants to sort of mentor me...further my career...'

'Wow! That's a change of heart!' Sheila frowned as she considered this unexpected news. 'I suppose that can only be a good thing. It'll help you get where you deserve. You're making quite a name for yourself. The sky's the limit and some help from the top can't be bad. A lot of people rate you. And they don't know half of what I know...' And her hand slipped down his body again, very suggestively.

Ken smiled ruefully. 'It's what she wants in return. A pound of flesh!'

Her hand found his penis. 'Well,' she purred, 'as long as it's not the pound I'm holding now...'

He wriggled. 'She wants me to open an

investigation into her boss. His expense claims. She thinks he's been less than honest on some of his claims.'

'And has he?'

'Possibly. It could amount to a misconduct charge. She thinks she'll get promoted in his place – if only as a temporary appointment.'

'It's not your area, is it? Fraud?'

'No. That's part of what's worrying me. She thinks I'll get involved because she' marked me down as a man who'll root out wrongdoing in the force.'

'And you have.'

'Yes, but not like this. Racism, misogyny, violence against women, gross misconduct - yes. I think these have no place in a modern force that's here to serve the whole of society. Matters of principle. Things worth putting myself on the line for. Risking the anger of fellow officers...'

'But she wants your help with this – a relatively minor matter. And in return...?'

'She hints that she'll foster my career once she's in control. I help her up the ladder and then there'll be payback.'

Sheila considered this. 'Well, why not? If there's been a real offence committed, it's perfectly reasonable to investigate it. If it helps you to get the promotion you deserve, then do it. More status, more salary, what's not to like?' But by then Ken's body had responded as expected to the hand that was stroking a very sensitive place. All discussion stopped in favour of very vigorous and satisfying sex. But after, when Sheila was slumbering beside him, Ken found it difficult to fall asleep. Sheila's words kept drifting through his mind. He hadn't realised just how status conscious she was. How, well, mercenary. It was disturbing. Doubts about her, that he had managed to suppress, began to resurface.

The next morning, he drove to the BBC studio in Southampton, consciously pushing all concerns out of his mind and concentrating on the interview to come. En route, a call from Hampshire CID brought him up to date on the ferry murder. Forensics had found traces of Jason's DNA and fingerprints in the cabin. The boy had taken his solicitor's advice and admitted his part in the killing, on the understanding that the court would be sympathetic, taking account of his age, his confession, and the cruelty he'd suffered. Olivia still insisted she was innocent of all charges, but the fact that she'd purchased her son's passage on the ship while insisting that he was still at home and attending school was proof enough, the Crown Prosecutors believed.

Good news, but it did little to lighten his mood. He wasn't looking forward to this television appearance. His new image as a champion of women's rights was becoming too much. In reception he met a young man from PR he didn't know and the force solicitor, Hilary Bedson. They had met before and had a quick embrace and kiss on the cheek. She was dressed as conservatively as the last time they'd met, in a dark trouser suit and white blouse. His first impression had not been positive. Her large, white-framed glasses, straw coloured hair and pale eyes had belied a sharp intelligence that he had come to respect. He had watched in silence as she destroyed the IOPC's case against him only a week ago, when they were accusing him of colluding with a pair of sex workers to attack two plain clothed officers. It had been the latter who had been in the wrong for demanding sex with menaces from the two women, and Hilary had been a power of strength in his defence. She pointed to a couple of sofas and they sat.

'Good to see you again, Ken.' She smiled enigmatically. 'And good you're not in trouble this time!'

'For the time being,' Ken replied.

'Well let's keep it that way, shall we? They'll want to talk to you about your childhood, why you are so aware of women's issues, so protective of them. No problem there, I think. When they move on to the action you've taken on police officers who offend, the force wants you to explain briefly, but not go into detail. We'll be with you, just out of shot. You understand it's important that you give the impression these were a few – a very few – bad apples. That the vast majority of the force is free from misogyny or racism. If you're tricked into a slip up, we'll step in straight away and stop the recording. We'll make sure the final edit follows our guidelines. So relax. You'll be fine.'

Ken grunted. He felt far from fine. This was the last thing he wanted – to be featured on national television. He hated publicity. And he felt even more uncomfortable when he was called into a dressing room for make-up. A lady in her early forties, she told him she was called Helen, led him into a small room with a very large mirror surrounded by light bulbs. The brightness hurt his eyes at first. She began by applying a neutral base cream to his face. He squirmed in embarrassment, partly from the unexpected intimacy of the fingers of an unknown person stroking his face and in part from the whole idea of being made up. It was something he'd never contemplated before. The make-up artist was immediately conscious of his discomfort. 'It's got to be done, dear. If we didn't apply a little colour, you'd look deathly white on screen. The lights in the studio are super bright. Just relax. You'll feel weird now, but on tv you'll look your normal handsome self!'

Now Ken's eyes had adjusted to the glare, he was able to look at Helen properly. She was wearing what looked to him like a kind of pale green smock. It was to protect her clothes from the powders and paints that were her stock in trade. She was slim, about 5 feet four, and he thought quite pretty. Auburn hair – he was far too ignorant of hair colouring to tell whether it was her natural colour. A cute nose, slightly turned up. As she moved to work on his eye lids, her face was very close to his. A nice feeling. She was, he decided, brisk and professional – qualities he admired. He closed his eyes and began to relax as she pampered him.

Then he realised that she was working more and more slowly. He idly wondered if this was her normal pattern. After a minute he opened his eyes and found that she was staring at him. 'Can I ask you something? Would you mind?' she asked, shyly.

He blinked. 'Course. Anything.' Then he had a surge of panic. Was she going to ask for his number? Or a date? 'Is it something professional… about my job?' He was relieved when she nodded. She stood in front of him with a cotton bud poised, her hand trembling slightly, as if this was a matter of great importance.

'I've heard a bit about why you're here. Why they want to talk to you. You're a great detective…' He shook his head. 'And you care about women's rights – stick up for us!' Ken said nothing. He waited. 'I wondered, if you have any time, I know it's a lot to ask…'

Ken smiled at her. 'Come on. Out with it.'

Helen sat in the chair opposite and gathered her thoughts. 'It was six years ago. Almost. They never found her. I don't know where she is. The police just seemed to give up – so easily!'

Ken sat up. 'Who was it? Someone important to you?'

She nodded. 'My sister - my younger sister - just before her eighteenth birthday. She left the house to meet some friends and just...disappeared. When she wasn't back the next morning, we called the police. They didn't seem to take it seriously. Took statements, then said she must have left home. Lots of teenagers do it. She'd probably come back eventually. Well – it's been six years and there's been nothing. And we were so close. She'd have been in touch – called me, text me. Why wouldn't she?'

Ken nodded sympathetically. 'It was a long time ago. Do you remember the name of the officer who was dealing with it?'

She furrowed her brow. 'I only met him twice. Long something. Longfellow?'

Alarm bells rang in Ken's head. 'Was it Longbottom? Detective Inspector Longbottom?'

Her eyes lit up. 'Yes! You know him?' Ken did. He'd been Longbottom's sergeant when he moved to Dorset. His boss had been close to retirement and, Ken knew, had lost any sharpness he might have had. A year and a half ago, when they were called to the woods near Bishop Farthing following the discovery of a body, Longbottom was certain that it was a natural death. It was clear to Ken that his superior just wanted to make life easy and avoid the trouble of a long investigation. It was only when Ken turned the body over and revealed a large hole in the chest that it became clear they were investigating a murder.

'When time passed and you didn't hear from her, did you contact the police again?'

The woman shrugged. 'The answer was always the same. People leave home. They don't always want to be found.'

Ken was stunned. He struggled not to sound disloyal to a retired officer. 'That sounds…as if you've still got lots of questions.' She nodded vigorously. He realised he didn't even know her surname. 'I'll look into it, I promise. If I can find out anything…there may be nothing…it's a long time ago…'

Her eyes shone. 'I'd be so grateful! Anything you can tell us! It's not knowing…'

'Of course. I'll need her name – and yours – and the address, where you were living at the time…'

'We still are. In Sherborne. Well, just outside.'

Ken nodded. Property in Sherborne is expensive. Just outside makes more sense. Before he could respond, there was a knock, and he was ushered through to the studio for the start of recording. Ken followed obediently but in better heart. It seemed to him that things were looking up. He still had to get through the interview but, after that, he had a real case to get his teeth into. A cold case as well – always intriguing. And even better – if he were involved in a complex investigation, he could hardly be expected to spare the time to follow up the Assistant Chief's quibble over her boss's expenses. There was a lightness in his step and a sparkle in his eye. His problems seemed to be over at last – both with his work and in his personal life!

Unknown to him, back at headquarters, he was about to gain assistance from an unlikely source. Jane, the Chief's loyal PA, was at that moment staring in confusion at the leather-bound diary. She had opened it at the last week in November, but the spine had been stretched and the book flopped open. She treated this volume with enormous respect. How could this have happened? Matters grew worse as she looked further back in the book. Page after page had been strained - opened far too wide so that the spine was giving way. Then she remembered that it had been borrowed by the ACC. So this was when the damage had happened. But how? And why? The book had been stretched apart as of it had been levelled on the glass of a photocopier. Jane turned to the sheets of expenses that Alicia had also borrowed. To her astonishment, she saw that one of the pages was not the original, signed off by the ACC and returned to her, but a photocopy. Alicia had copied every sheet, but in her hurry to return them to Jane had not noticed that one of the sheets was the copy she had made.

Jane was not only loyal, and perhaps loving, but also exceptionally intelligent. Like many women in her position, she kept her true abilities under wraps; happy to serve and content to be simply very good at her job. But now, her mind was working overtime. She checked the expenses against the diary entries that Alicia had copied. It slowly dawned on Jane that Alicia had been checking one against the other. A quick glance showed her that some of the entries could be open to...misinterpretation. With a sickening jolt she realised what Alicia was up to. It was not only loyalty that drove Jane to protect her boss from over-rigorous analysis of his expense claims. Alicia's assumption that he was using the excess to fund speculative purchases on the stock exchange was wide of the mark. Jane knew that he had a private bank account, unknown to his wife, that he could use to finance weekends away with Jane and the occasional very special gift.

Shaking with rage, she took the evidence into her boss. At first, he found it hard to understand. But once he understood what his assistant was planning, he too was furious.

Alicia was summoned. At first, she denied

any wrongdoing. But when she was ordered to bring the file with the copies she'd made without permission, her defence crumpled. As Ken completed his ordeal in front of the cameras, his nemesis was facing suspension from duty. If Ken had known, he would have been doubly pleased. He'd be able to carry out his work without the ACC towering over him and he was enjoying the love of a beautiful woman. Life was looking good.

But he couldn't have been more wrong. Life was about to get very complicated. And Ken would find himself on a case stranger and more mysterious than he could ever imagine...

Look out for the next book in the DI Jones series to find out what happens!

For more information on female psychopaths, read the work of Dr Clive Boddy of Anglia-Ruskin University. He argues that we have failed to recognise female psychopaths because so much of the research has been done on men in prison for violent crimes. Most psychopaths are actually living apparently successful lives by using their personality traits to deceive and manipulate - even bully - those around them. They could be anywhere. We could meet them at work, socially, or in politics... So beware - there could be one near you!

ABOUT THE AUTHOR

Paul Cosway

Paul lives in Dorset with his wife,  Maureen, and their dog, Toby - along with chickens and a pond full of fish. He loves gardening; collects old toys; builds model raiways; paints and writes stories for adults and children, poetry and articles. He cares passionately about women's rights and unfairmess of all kinds. These are themes that run through all his books.

BOOKS BY THIS AUTHOR

Bishop Farthing

A funny and touching love story set during the covid lockdown!

Don't Go Down To The Woods Today!

The first of the Ken Jones stories. A body is found in the bluebell woods at Bishop Farthing and Ken finds himself dealing with an organised crime syndicate involved in trafficking, prostitution and money laundering. Oh - and his love life isn't going smoothly either!

Death In Retreat!

The naked body of a woman is found in the grounds of a Christian Retreat. Ken has his doubts about the self-styled prophet who is running the place. But before he can complete his investigation a baby is reported stolen. Another amazing story, definitely for adults, full of intrigue, humour and romance!

Death Or Dishonour!

Most mysterious...the bodies of chldren are uncovered in a cottage garden. Ken is tasked with discovering who they were, how they died and who killed them! It's a thrill ride as he struggles to bring the guilty to justice and the result is an exciting and gripping story full of relevance today!

All these titles are available as ebooks or paperback books from Amazon and selected booksellers.

Printed in Great Britain
by Amazon